GOODNESS

GOODNESS

TIM PARKS

GROVE WEIDENFELD
New York

Published by Grove Weidenfeld
A division of Grove Press, Inc.
841 Broadway
New York, NY 10003-4793

First published in Great Britain in 1991 by William Heinemann Ltd., London.

Library of Congress Cataloging-in-Publication Data

Parks, Tim.
    Goodness/Tim Parks—1st American ed.
      p.   cm.
    "First published in Great Britain in 1991
by William Heinemann Ltd."—T.p. verso.
    ISBN 0-8021-1390-7
    I. Title.
    PR6066.A6957G6   1991   91-21937
    823'.914—dc20   CIP

Manufactured in the United States of America

Printed on acid-free paper

First American Edition 1991

10 9 8 7 6 5 4 3 2 1

GOODNESS

Prologue

My father was a missionary murdered in Burundi in 1956. It was very much his own fault. He had been warned to leave and by not doing so he risked getting the rest of us killed too. When we were captured in our white mission bungalow, my mother, my sister and I were given the choice of dying with him or of saying some simple formula that renounced our faith, after which we would be allowed to leave the country. I was too young of course either to have a faith or to renounce it, though I don't doubt what my decision would have been. My mother on the other hand was torn. She's a superstitious woman and believes in the power of words spoken even when not meant, the kind of person who would feel guilty at discovering that the phrase she had innocently repeated in some foreign language was blasphemy. Even today she wonders if she won't be punished for all eternity for having responded to her maternal instinct and saved both herself and us.

It's curious thinking about this now. Presumably a shot rang out and dispatched my father. I don't remember, I was too small. I haven't the slightest memory either of him or of Africa. If I think of his martyrdom at all it is with total incomprehension. And if I mention the grotesque affair now it is only because over the years I have come to see it as just the first, the most absurdly emblematic, of a long series of incidents in which other people's pretensions to goodness were to clash, to my considerable detriment, with the most naked common sense.

Part One

BEFORE
HILARY

A Bundle of
Unpleasant Contradictions

After my father's death we came back to England to live with my widowed grandfather and spinster aunt in an ill-conceived semi-detached in Park Royal, about mid way between the Middlesex Hospital and where they later built the A40. My grandfather, who had escaped his country labourer background with a naval career that pulled him up to the dizzy heights of home ownership, lace curtains, embossed wallpaper and the like, was of the opinion that he was doing us a great favour putting a roof over our heads, and having never been able to stomach my fervently evangelical father, adopted a told-you-so attitude that was to weigh heavily on my sister Peggy and myself throughout our childhood, and even more so, one imagines, on my mother who had no money to go elsewhere.

'Those jungle boys,' the old man would begin, though I don't suppose he could have been much over fifty then, 'haven't got souls to save, have they?' He smoked a pipe, as grandfathers will, or used to, and regularly occupied a heavy shapeless armchair in an ungenerous living room choked with green Wedgewood and Hummels. 'Never saw the point of missionarying,' he grunted.

I remember, from where I would be lying on the hearthrug, being fascinated by his facial skin, especially on the cheeks where the pores were so thick and large as to suggest the texture of some old neglected sponge. Certainly they had soaked up enough in their time. His hair was already white and prickly short, the kind old men scratch vigorously. 'Shifty sods too.' He sucked in through his nose. 'Saw enough of that lot in my time to know to leave well alone, I did.'

Naturally he was speaking, even in those early days, over the urgent clamour of the television which he watched fixedly but didn't appear to need to listen to. Unless it was encroaching deafness. He puffed one pipe while scraping the bowl of another. 'If Arthur'd had any sense at all he'd have kept a gun in the house. Couple of loud bangs would have had that lot scarpering. That's what I say.'

My mother only said. 'Please, Dad. Please,' and would get up and go into the kitchen. He might shout after her: 'For God's sake, Jenny, can't you even take a joke? Or are you going to mourn after him your whole bloody life?' She wouldn't answer. She would never answer. This is my mother's way. For my own part, I remember feeling desperately sorry for her, yet incapable of intervening, since I always suspected that Grandfather, incorrigibly unpleasant and offensive as he was, was right. What was the point of missionarying? What possible sense did it make? My father must have been mad to go out there talking to blacks with their bones in their noses, their drums, their funny clothes, when they wore them (we had photographs). It wasn't that I was of an age to hold any progressive beliefs on the equal value of all cultures and religions. Quite the contrary. Just that somehow, from the cradle, I didn't believe in the saving and transformation of souls. My intuition has always been that people are who they are and forever remain so, or at best will simply become more and more themselves, more and more that spirit that you can't help but feel destined to be. Just as it is destiny to be black, destiny to be white. This is what self means, surely. Otherwise who are we?

Only Peggy objected. Only she stood up for Father. She said: 'You shouldn't say those kinds of things, Grandad.' We sat, lay, stood in that smoky suburban sitting room in West London: floral carpet, a pattern of coronation crowns and sceptres on the wallpaper, the grey TV carelessly wrapping and rewrapping time into odd half hours of this and that. Peggy said: 'Black people have souls just like us. Yes they do. Red and yellow, black and white, all are precious in His sight.'

What would she have been, seven, nine? She wore her hair in a ponytail and stood chubbily round-bottomed by Grandfather's chair. She said: 'Daddy was a good man. He loved the Lord Jesus and he wanted to save people so they wouldn't go to hell. And now he has gone to heaven to wait for us there.'

While she spoke of course, my Grandfather would keep mumbling and rumbling his prejudices, since this wasn't really a conversation so much as two people at either end of life speaking their parts in each other's presence. 'Man would've done better if he'd thought of his own wife and kids before those bloody chimpanzees.'

I might catch the sound of my mother crying softly in the kitchen.

'God is looking after us,' Peggy insisted.

'With the help of muggins here's pension I suppose,' Grandfather came back. Until eventually he turned from the television to look at her out of sunken brown eyes. Though there was still a glint there. He would have been wearing his pub-going dark waistcoat, shirt-sleeves rolled up; a bulky, heavy-breathing presence.

Staring him out, she said: 'Don't be such a miserable old grumbler, Grandad. It's sinful to grumble and be miserable.'

The sight of her, rather than anything she said, would at last make him forget his racist grouching. He'd say, 'Come here, Peggy love. Come and sit on Grandad's knee.'

She pouted. She might well have had her hands on her hips. Probably she was already aware of striking poses. Certainly Grandfather recognised them when they were struck. He liked to grab her and cuddle her hard on his knee and say things like: 'My jewel, my Peggy. I do like a little girlie with some sparkle about her.'

My mother cooked, Grandfather rowed with or cuddled Peggy, and around six thirty Aunt Mavis came back, flopped down in an armchair, kicked off her shoes, treating us to a whiff of feet which nobody commented on, and lit a cigarette. I even remember the brand, Park Drive. They

7

were the first I tried myself, stealing from her handbag. With her and Grandad together and the windows forever closed against 'the damp', we thus sat out the 1960s in a thick Virginia smog.

Very quietly, to myself and Peggy, when she had us on our own walking to church perhaps, my mother would say: 'Smoking is evil. Because it's an abuse of the body the Lord gave you.' It was the nearest she came to criticising Grandfather openly. She said: 'Our bodies are precious, holy. Every human body, His temple, made in His image. That's why you must never smoke. You must promise me you'll never smoke.' I suppose one might have objected that martyrdom was an even greater abuse of this image of God's we were supposed to be taking care of. But as a boy this never occurred and later there would seem no point in being cruel, since, come eighteen odd, you have learnt to humour rather than rebel. You have already won your freedom. Or at least you're of an age to think in such terms.

In line with her firm belief in the holiness of the human body, my mother wore no make-up, no earrings, no jewels at all apart from her wedding and engagement ring; she was a well-built, auburn, rather attractive woman, I suppose, with a pale quiet intense energy. Her sister, Aunt Mavis, on the other hand, made up heavily and did everything to hair and skin that the fashions of each season dictated. Barely two years younger than my mother, she nevertheless affected the manner and aspirations of the teenage factory girls she worked with. I remember her, well into her thirties she must have been, still talking to us with adolescent dreaminess of Mr Right and the very large family she intended to have, when quite probably she had never so much as been kissed. She was ugly. Her features were oddly flat, she had no chin, and there was something out of true about her eyes, so that only one ever appeared to be looking directly at you.

As I grew older I began to appreciate that Aunt Mavis was a figure of fun, even ridicule. She said things out of the blue, laughed when there seemed no reason to, or alternatively cried. At nine or ten perhaps I began to feel seriously embarrassed about her, especially if I brought friends home, embarrassed that she was part of our family at all. It seemed so extraordinary, this having to accept the imposition of people you weren't comfortable with. Forever chattering and clapping her hands, forever retailing the small change of factory gossip, a curiously vacant expression hovered about Aunt Mavis's flattened features, a disturbing lack of focus. She wasn't a normal person. Apart from the television, she dedicated most of her spare time to the Harrow branch of the Elvis Presley Fan Club, of which she claimed to have been a founder member. And perhaps she was. It was inane enough. All I know is that as she chunnered on and on, always senseless, always excited, full of affected gestures and expressions which often she misunderstood, I simply wished and wished she would disappear.

Twenty years later, during the months of guerilla warfare that tore the heart out of our marriage, I remember Shirley telling me that I had been entirely conditioned by this family of mine, that I had just soaked up the pathetic piety of my mother, the coarseness of my grandfather, the amorality of my sister, and a fair dose of poor Aunt Mavis's dumbness too. These are the kinds of things one says in arguments, I suppose, and my own feeling is that nothing could be further from the truth. What kind of combination would that be? Piety, coarseness, amorality?

'They don't mix,' I told her.

'Dead right,' she said, 'you're a bundle of contradictions, George Crawley, and unpleasant ones at that.'

But those were the good old days, pre-Hilary. I can't recall Shirley and me arguing in quite the same aimless, indulgent way afterwards.

Walking Wounded

My mother led a strange life. At home, in Gorst Road, she was little more than a slave. Even Aunt Mavis used to demand things of her, would say: 'I'm the modern woman, aren't I? Bringing home the bread, the least I can expect is to have my bed made for me.' She blinked, gormless and vapid.

Mother bowed to it. She did everything, shopped, cooked, washed up, cleaned, mended, gardened, darned, scrubbed, laundered, ironed. She was always tired, her skin always rough with work. And it occurs to me that apart from the brief interlude of her marriage, of Africa, she had been doing more or less the same thing in the same house since her early teens when her own mother died. For all of which she received no pay and less thanks, not a person who didn't take her for granted.

Yet the curious thing was that at our church, the local Methodists, Mother was a figure of considerable importance: a taker of meetings, reader of lessons, organiser of conferences and outings; a woman of quick decision, easy authority and loud, strong singing voice. We sang, 'He who would valiant be,' and she was booming and triumphant. For Father had been valiant. We sang, 'For all the saints, who from their labours rest,' and she had tears in her eyes, thinking of the saint my father had been, the rest he had deserved.

She was much loved, even revered. People came to her with their problems. They came with the most intimate problems, the most serious, even legal problems. For them she was both comfort and oracle. People came and wept with her, prayed with her, told everything. I always found, and to this day still do find, this fact extraordinary. I myself was unable to talk to my mother about anything: about religion, about my own wilderness of doubt, about my dead father, about Grandfather's unpleasantness, about Aunt Mavis's queerness, most of all about puberty (Peggy's an explosion, physical and behavioural, my own slower, more furtive and guilty, later bold and deceitful). I was unable to talk to her about anything, and she in turn made no attempt to tackle anything intimate with me, nor with Peggy, who, through her friends at school, became my chief source of the vital information one inevitably grubs around for at that age.

I remember looking in Mother's handbag. I was supposed to be getting change for collection. She wasn't going to church for some reason. She had problems with her hips sometimes. Bouts of something or other. And ferreting for her purse amidst a mess of hankies, keys and scraps of paper, breathing the forever memorable, blown-nose and old-leather smell of her bag, I came across a tampon, a cylinder wrapped in ricepaper. I said: 'What's this, Mum?' At once she was flustered. I latched on immediately. 'What is it?' I said. 'Put it away.' 'But what is it, Mum?'

You would have thought, looking back, here was her opportunity to give young George his lesson, to guide him towards some mature understanding of the female body. But no, she says: 'It's a cigar.' I couldn't swear, but this may be the only straight lie my mother ever told me. 'For Grandfather.'

I looked at the long tube in its flimsy paper cover. It looked the right shape for a cigar, the big ones they advertised with organ music on the box. I said: 'But you don't like Grandad to smoke.' 'For his birthday,' she wriggled. 'It's next Friday you know.' She found a painful smile. 'We can waive a rule for his birthday, can't we? Bless his dear heart.'

And I swallowed it. The extraordinary thing being that she then went out and actually bought a cigar for the old man's birthday. Odd, no, to think of my mother being so cunning, so resourceful in her prudishness? For what? To save my innocence? In a world where the worst is anyway chalked on every wall. In a family where, that very evening, Peggy had already told me everything, mocking my innocence, even showing me quite graphically (using a 'Q' tip) how you fitted them in.

Yet almost everybody in the church brought their problems to this woman, their confessions. They came to her after service in the hall where we had coffee and she would go off with them to the vestry, leaving Peggy and me to kick our heels in the yard amongst stacks of coal and tiles from the roof they'd had to remove because they were dangerous. They came to her at home in Gorst Road, sometimes late in the evening and she took them to her room. 'Here comes another of the walking wounded,' Grandfather would announce when the bell ding-donged in the middle of the *Man from Uncle*, *Harry Worth's Half Hour*. 'Out with the bandages. Call the nurse. Or is it to be last rites?' And when one Saturday afternoon a black came, he said with his extraordinary flair for insensitivity: 'Don't you think we should frisk him? Don't want any trouble.'

But despite his prejudices and scorn Grandfather never actually prevented anybody from coming in. Even the most dishevelled of tramps (for Mother was famous for giving tea to vagrants in the kitchen – 'Four sugars, ma'am'); even, as the sixties progressed, the occasional Indian (if Grandfather despised blacks, he truly loathed Indians). And this was another thing with my mother, that however much derision she attracted, and probably still attracts, she generally gets her way; and even if she doesn't answer back, she has a quiet authority in her passivity, a power really, something terribly persuasive about her softly focusing brown eyes. Charisma. It was her 'ministry'.

'My ministry,' I heard her explaining when she turned down Eddie Foulkes who owned the Hallmarks Plastics factory on Bowes Road and always put a tenner in the collection plate. I was on hands and knees on threadbare carpet in the dark light at the top of the stairs. They were by the porch below. She had prayed about it and the Lord had told her no.

Grandfather was furious when I told him and there was

the most almighty row. She was putting her prayer rubbish before the welfare of her bloody family. Wasn't it enough that her husband had been killed by a bunch of nignogs? Wasn't it enough that she lived on the social, that we couldn't afford decent clothes? Mother said Eddie had been divorced, she could never marry a man who had broken a solemn vow to someone else. Otherwise what did promises mean? Grandfather was livid. He spat. Peggy said everybody got divorced and she couldn't see the problem, especially seeing as they liked each other. Eddie was fab. Mother didn't cry; Mother only cried when she was afraid for your soul. 'Maybe if *I* stayed at home and did nothin' all day *I*'d 'ave more of a chance of getting married,' Mavis said.

It was a nasty scene and partly my fault, since I had hoped the others would be able to change her mind and we could move into Eddie's big house over in Ealing. Also I honestly believed it would be the best thing for my mother. Grandfather raved on and on. I seem to remember it was on this occasion that he hit her. When the whole thing got too painful I went out the back and kicked a ball against the wall. I decided that after I had escaped my family and was in control of my life, I would never be gratuitously mean or violent, as Grandfather was, but then nor would I ever put up with anybody or any situation that made life unbearable, as Mother did. I would be honest and reasonable, generous where generosity was due, and I would always always choose the road that led to a happy, healthy, normal life.

Wasn't that a fair stab at a moral code? For a fourteen-year-old. And one I honestly do believe I've stuck to.

Although only a month or so ago, when she found my scrapbook, Shirley said: 'You are aware you're not human, aren't you? You are aware of that? Because I know what you're thinking.'

'Only too human,' I replied, 'to go by what's in those papers.'

But Shirley had become one of the walking wounded herself by this time.

A Certain Grace

Aunt Mavis finally found her Mr Right. Bob Hare was about ten years her younger, unemployed, slim to the point of frail and a Mormon. When he spoke it was with the extreme and unfriendly caution of somebody who is not expecting a fair trial. 'Oh, God,' Grandad announced after his first visit, 'a turd on two legs. And I thought I'd seen it all.'

Bob spent his days proselytising on doorsteps in Shepherd's Bush and Holland Park. Although timid, he was obviously grimly determined, constantly summoning up all his courage to get a foot in the door and jabber out his lines: the Book of Mormon, the moral decay of our society, the only road to salvation, the importance of the family, what have you. Naturally the reaction he was most at home with was rebuff. He drew the dole and rent relief, which disgusted my grandfather, and was unhealthily pale and sickly-looking in a pinched, persecuted way. If he had any attraction at all it was that haunted and haunting, thin-boned, soft-eyed passion you often find in black-and-white photos of refugees and general strikers. Mother saw red, though she was careful to call him 'Poor dear Bob'. Aunt Mavis was having none of it and after only a couple of months married him without telling any of us, so that late one Saturday afternoon, there she was, tubby in tight slacks, gathering her clobber together and setting off for a bedsit in Haringey.

Where very soon she miscarried. Not once but twice. This much I learnt from Peggy who had overheard a conversation between Mother and Grandfather. Mother, who blamed herself terribly for this injudicious marriage and visited regularly, asked me to come with her to cheer Mavis up, telling me only that she was depressed. I refused. My mother insisted. Why should I? I asked. Had Mavis ever come to see me? Perhaps I was just annoyed that at sixteen or seventeen, or whatever I now was, I still wasn't to be let in on the serious and intimate information in the family, I was being treated like a child, my opinion wasn't required. I told her I wouldn't go unless Mavis asked me herself. Mother said this attitude was unchristian of me and selfish. I pointed out that no one else was being asked to go, not Peggy, not Grandfather. 'We can go into town afterwards,' she pleaded, 'perhaps treat you to something you want to see.' For it was and still is so important to Mother that an appearance of family solidarity be kept up.

We took two long London bus-rides through depressing streets, the new estates that were already slums. There was a terraced house, four flights of uncarpeted stairs, a dingy yellow door where a rag did for a doormat and a note said: 'Bell don't work. Knock.'

I blame my mother really for never finding out more about Mavis and what was wrong with her. I mean, it's one thing being good and generous to all and sundry, but my own feeling is that we have certain strategic responsibilities to the members of our family that are far more important. Mavis was obviously not quite right in the head. One knew that if only from the way people instinctively treated her with condescension, not unkindly, but with indulgence rather, the way you treat animals, half-wits, tiny babies. Yet my mother never enquired into what might lie behind this. I have no memory of any doctor ever being invited to pronounce on her odd facial features or retarded mental development. She was just accepted from the start for what she was, dumb, childish, ugly. And while it's all very well saying we're all God's creatures whatever's the matter with us, I do believe that Mother failed in her duty here.

Bob was out to see the social security people. Mavis was in bed, eating sweets, smoking. Fishing for a piece of toffee stuck to her teeth, she talked about her miscarriages quite openly in my presence, despite initial frowns and signs of discouragement from my mother. Mother asked had the doctors said anything about why, and Mavis laughed and said, nothing that made any sense. She blew out smoke through one nostril and then the other. She and Bob were determined she said. They had mostly got married for the kids. He was mad about them.

I wanted to go because of the smell, the unpleasantness, and then the embarrassing inanity of my aunt's twitter. She was showing some baby clothes she had bought now. She was sure it was going to be a boy. She giggled. When it finally decided to turn up. I remember her big pear-shaped body heaving from one side of the bed to another to pick things up off the floor; she let out grunts, her cigarette flecking the blankets with ash. I was desperate to go, I get quite frantic sometimes when I find myself in unpleasant situations, I simply can't bear it, I feel I will die of unpleasantness; but Mother of course felt duty bound to wash the dishes, hoover the carpet, save the unsaveable. I offered to help, to speed things up, but was told to keep Mavis company, drink my tea.

I stood by the bed with my hands in my pockets. I didn't want any tea and I had spent my whole childhood in the same house as Mavis without ever talking to her. Was it likely we would find anything to say to each other now? I told her we were going into town afterwards to see the Queen's stamp collection. I told her Peggy had got herself a dog but then never bothered to look after it, she was so busy playing the drums in a rock group all the time. Grandfather loathed the thing. I told her I was going to university in a year or two so as to be able to leave home. Mavis licked a thumb. I asked her if she liked being married, and she said it was all right and stopping work was the best thing that could ever have happened to her, not having to get up so early and have your hands ruined by those hot machines. 'Which reminds me,' she said. 'Where's me lipstick?'

Bob came back. He stood frail and knotty-haired in the doorway watching my mother down on her knees having a go at crud on the carpet. The room was quite big, maybe fifteen by fifteen, but it had everything, kitchenette, bed, table, chairs, sofa, so it was cluttered, with just the one orange-curtained window and a busy road behind to rattle it.

'No need to do that,' he said brusquely. 'I'd have done that.'

When he got closer to us you couldn't not be aware he'd been drinking. He looked belligerent, ready to snap.

'We clean the place every day,' he insisted. His eyes were pink.

Preparing to leave, Mother made a whole pantomine of signs with her eyes for him to come outside and have a word about Mavis. A rock would have understood, but Bob's strained face merely filled with puzzlement. I was tugging at Mother's coat cuff to be gone. Mavis was propped up in bed staring chinlessly. How old must she have been? Thirty-six? Thirty-eight? Mother made her signs again. Perhaps half understanding, Bob said: 'We're okay. We don't need help from no one.' He was tense.

'Cheerie bye,' Mother called past him to her sister. At the corner of the stairs we heard raised voices above us. Shouting. Mother hesitated one short second in mid step, then quickened her pace.

With what relief I let myself out into the street and took a breath of fresh air! I had hurried on ahead. For life, as I have so often insisted to Shirley of late, should have a certain grace, shouldn't it? A certain grace. Please. Otherwise I do believe one might as well be dead.

A Classic Case

The first time I threw in my weight in an attempt to tip the scales toward sanity and common sense was on the occasion of Peggy's first pregnancy. I would have been living in Leicester by then. Shirley and I had moved in together, having found ourselves quite a decent semi some miles from the university; it was pricey, but we shared with a couple of other students and Mr Harcourt, her father, unwittingly provided what I couldn't always afford.

It would be difficult to exaggerate what a release this change of scene was, how wonderful at last, at last, not to have to worry that Mother would find out what one was up to, not to have to face her silent and suffering reproach, her insistent, if never spoken, 'Be thou me! Be thou me!' I didn't go back home from one end of term to the other and certainly not for such minor events as Grandfather's prostectomy or Aunt Mavis's suicide attempt. Mother wrote asking me to come and I wrote back asking what possible help could I be, and explaining that the important thing for me surely was to get the best degree possible and so escape the poverty trap that in the future world of high technology and high unemployment people from my sort of unskilled lower middle-class background were in every danger of falling into.

Mother wrote to say she understood, though it would be nice if I could make it home just sometimes, and she kept me up to date on such events as the death of Peggy's dog Jagger (fed chicken bones by Grandfather), the church meetings she spoke at, what she had cooked when so and so and so and so, who were missionaries in Borneo or clergymen from Nigeria, had come to lunch, her contacts with Peggy (scrubbing clean some slum my sister was squatting in, lending her ten pounds she would never see again), stories of a stray cat she had taken in, a tramp she had fed who had walked off with Grandfather's favourite lighter, so and so who had been converted when so and so came to speak to the youth fellowship, conversations with the next door neighbours about the state of the sewage pipes under the garden, our sycamore that took light from their front room, the rotting fence they wanted to fix and Mother couldn't afford to, etc. etc.

I didn't go home. I was happy as I had never been before: work, play, parties, independence, self-indulgence, Shirley. Until mid way through the third year Mother sent a telegram: 'Peggy in family way, please please come.'

It was a classic case of people not doing what was most sensible and convenient for everybody concerned, and thus a forerunner of events to come. Worth dwelling on. Mavis, I discovered on arrival home (Mother's letters were clearly rather less informative than they liked to present themselves), had come back to live in Gorst Road after swallowing a half bottle of bleach. Her second attempt. Bringing only the minimum dole with her, she spent her days listening to old Elvis Presley records in her room and whining about Bob who had now left the Mormons and joined some Eastern fringe religion based in Indonesia and run by a charismatic figure known as the Bapi. This had disorientated Mavis. The Bapi had ordered Bob, as he did all his converts, to take a new name. So Bob was now Raschid. The root cause of their break-up had apparently been that Mavis, in a surprising show of independence, had infuriated Bob by refusing to call him Raschid or to contemplate changing her own name. She was Mavis and she liked to be called Mavis. I suppose the only positive thing about all this was that it was a good story to tell at dinner parties. Financially it was a disaster.

Peggy meanwhile had been squatting in Islington playing drums in a small folk group and helping in a War on Want shop on Camden High Street which had been raided for drugs on three occasions. Thrown out of the squat a few days before, she had temporarily returned home, more to make a visit than out of any real need for refuge, since Peggy could have found a bed at a moment's notice almost anywhere in the city, so extensive was and is her network of friends, or rather of those people who immediately recognise in her one of their own subculture.

She came home and over tea quite by the way and without the slightest sense of momentousness, told Mother that she was pregnant. Later in the same conversation, throughout which Mother had with her customary infinite caution been trying to find out more, Peggy asked her for a large, indeed by our family standards huge, sum of money, without specifying why she needed it. At which Mother had quickly put an old-fashioned two and two together and telegrammed me.

I arrived in the afternoon towards three. In a clearly agitated state, so unlike the serene air of wisdom she would offer her walking wounded, Mother caught me at the door before I could ring the bell, so as to grab a private word: she had stalled Peggy over the issue of the money, she said, though in reality she could never afford such a sum. She had stalled her to prevent her from going elsewhere before I arrived. She wanted me to talk to her rather than doing it herself because she knew Peggy considered her something of a religious fuddy duddy whereas coming from me the advice would have much more authority. Peggy respected me. She was always saying how much common sense I had and how well I was doing. And of course I was young. Everybody set so much store by what generation you belonged to these days. I must tell her that it was wrong to have an abortion. Quite wrong. It was killing a child. It was murder. There was nothing more one could say about it and all the modern arguments in its favour were just unadulterated institutionalised selfishness. How could they be anything but? A child was alive and you killed it, and it was so shameful that something that called itself the women's movement supported such carnage. Peggy must have the baby. She must. If she didn't want it afterwards, Mother herself would keep it. Something somehow could always be arranged. There were so many people wanted babies and couldn't have them.

I was a shade overwhelmed. Every day, or at least every month of her life in her role as self-appointed social worker Mother must have dealt with more or less similar situations; she'd had plenty of girls from the church come to her pregnant by the wrong man, or by the right man at the wrong time. Yet her sense of urgency now, her determination to persuade, was extraordinary. The wrinkled corners of her soft mouth trembled. Her hands were clasped together with unnatural force. Her living soul-self seemed to be concentrated in the fluttering, watering eyes looking at me so intensely. You could see how for her, for my mother, a simple suburban abortion was raised to the level of a vast metaphysical showdown between good and evil. There were angels and demons perched all over the furniture.

'Please, George,' she said. 'Please.'

Fresh, or rather stale, from coach and tube, still struggling a little to reaccustom myself to the prayer-meeting rhetoric, I pointed out that Peggy could hardly want the money for an abortion, since abortions, like it or not, were now free on the health service. Mother stopped. She was breathing quickly: 'Oh, of course. Of course. How stupid of me. How stupid!' And she asked: 'Is there any chance she doesn't know?'

Peggy apparently was out the back soaking up the year's first sunshine. I said I would go and talk to her, get to the bottom of it at once. 'Please,' Mother said again. 'Okay,' I said.

So far we had talked in undertones amidst the pungent shoe and old geranium smells of the porch, but now, crossing living room and kitchen to reach the back, I was struck as never before by the dinginess of my old home. The wallpaper was a glazed yellow brown, the carpet threadbare – a rug aslant, itself badly worn, rather obviously covering the hole by the passage door. Sofa and armchair with their washed out once elastic covers were more than ever tattered and shapeless.

I looked, and found it desperately poignant to think of my dear mother wasted in that unpromising environment. I felt a surge of moral energy. I was the success of the house. I was about to graduate. These people needed help and it was up to me to give it to them. Rather than staying away, I should be making regular visits to check the situation out, see what ought to be done.

I opened the back door. Outside was a twice folded handkerchief of lawn surrounded by rosebushes and other, for me nameless, flowers which my mother somehow found time to cultivate and water and worry about. They about half-hid the black creosoted fence that sagged behind. I stepped out, ducked under a line straining with damp washing, and found Peggy sprawled on a patch of dandelions in bra and pants, exposing her chunky pale body to sunshine that seemed barely warm. A scruffy little dog nobody had told me about was idly licking her ribs.

'Peggy.'

She sat up and broadly smiled surprise. 'You too!' she said. 'Quite a reunion. How nice.' Falling forward as her body came up, her breasts were plump. She stroked the little dog. 'Do you like Theo? He waylaid me on the Heath and refuses to go away.'

I pushed aside a damp green nylon sheet and squatted down. I paused. I said: 'Mother tells me you're pregnant.'

She was squinting still to adjust her eyes. 'Oh you've grown a moustache.' She burst out into one of her laughs. 'Makes you look a bit AC/DC.'

In a low voice, I explained that Mother had telegrammed for me to come down to persuade her not to have an abortion, but that in fact I was entirely on her side. Entirely. So not to worry. Of course she should have an abortion. The feminists were perfectly right. It was her body to do what she wanted with. It was her decision. If she went and had a baby now what kind of career could she ever expect to have? Not to mention the poor child growing up in these slummy surroundings, with not even much prospect of work at the end of the day, and then the present international climate, the threat of nuclear war and so on. Was it a world to bring kids into? I'd support her one hundred per cent if Mother started putting on any pressure, in fact I felt just about ready for a showdown, let her know what I thought about her repressive religious ideas, though seeing as it was really none of her business the best thing would be simply not to say anything and then to present her with a *fait accompli*. If she . . .

'But I don't want to have an abortion,' Peggy blinked.

I was taken aback. She leaned over and ruffled my hair. She kissed my cheek, playing older sister. 'Don't worry your little head about it, Georgie, you're so worked up, cool it, take it easy, I'll sort it all out myself, it's no problem.'

She smiled. Then she said: 'So poor Mum thought I was planning an abortion?' and she got up and ran into the house to tell Mother she had never had any intention of getting an abortion. Never. How on earth had she got that idea into her head? Oh, when she'd asked for money it was because she and some other friends were clubbing together to put up bail for one of the guys in the squat who'd been arrested. Completely trumped up drugs charges. The police should be ashamed of themselves. From the garden I could hear Mother weeping for joy, fierce hiccups of emotion, promising what funds she had.

Later, over tea and buns, which she insisted on baking and even icing as a sort of celebration, Mother asked: 'Not the father, I hope?'

'You what?' Peggy was licking her finger to pick up crumbs from her plate. Mavis fed herself vacantly.

'This fellow who's been arrested. He's not the father?'

'Oh no,' Peggy laughed.

I couldn't help feeling as we munched away that I was the only one there actually concerned about the practical implications of this development. I said: 'So maybe you wouldn't mind telling Mum who the father is, since she's probably going to have to look after the poor child.'

Peggy turned to me in surprise. 'Oh my, aren't we a sour puss!'

Mother said: 'George's only trying to help, dear. It was so nice of him to come down. Now do tell us about the chappie.'

'His name's Dave,' Peggy said. 'He's an actor, a wonderful man. We're going to get married as soon as we can. And we shall be looking after the child ourselves, thank you very much. Why ever shouldn't we?'

'Don't look at me,' Mavis came out in an inexplicable huff.

'I thought,' I said, 'that getting married was one of the few things you could do from one moment to the next if you really wanted to.'

'If you must know, brother dear,' Peggy said with condescending sweetness, 'we've got to wait until his divorce comes through.'

Typically my mother said nothing. She passed round the buns again, merely remarking that they hadn't risen as much as they might and she hadn't been able to fill them with buttercream as she usually did because there was only marge in the house these days and without running out to the shops . . . The fact that Peggy was plunging into the most precarious of situations (with an actor!), as a result of which Mother herself would suffer, certainly financially if in no other way, did not appear to worry her at all. She herself had refused to marry a perfectly decent and quite wealthy man ostensibly because he had divorced nearly a decade before, and now her daughter was having another man divorce to marry her and she didn't say anything about it, when some serious comment might just have made her see sense. As a result of which, I was being forced into a position where I had to be unpleasant simply to express the only sensible opinion possible.

'Seems to me,' I began, 'you're hardly . . .' But Mother caught the sound of the rotary sprinkler in the next garden and rushed out to pull in the washing. She preferred this to inviting our new neighbour, a vanguard of gentrification, to adjust the thing. No sooner was she out than Peggy leaned across the table towards me, her breasts swinging heavily: 'What's got into you, George?'

'What do you mean?'

'For heaven's sake! You seem to be doing your best to ruin a happy situation and start an argument. Relax. Please.' She was wearing earrings the size of saucers, punk dark lipstick.

I said: 'I'm sorry, Peggy, but I thought I was trying to prevent an unhappy situation from developing.'

And when Mother came back in I told her I was off. I'd take the coach back to Leicester that night. I had a lot of studying to do. At the door she thanked me, as if it had been me had worked the miracle. She embraced me and kissed me. In the background Grandfather was complaining to the TV about the influx of Kenyan Asians.

I wash my hands of you all, I thought.

Lucky Stars

What was it I liked so much about Shirley? Why did we become so rapidly and permanently attached? I can't rightly remember. At seventeen, eighteen, one is so much immersed in life. One likes without noticing quite what or why, in a whirl of vanity and self-gratification.

We met at a retreat intended to promote church unity. There must be an irony there. The well-to-do Anglo Caths in Chiswick High Street were dallying with the Shepherd's Bush Congregationalists and Park Royal Methodists, and the youth of the three churches were lured off to an Easter Week of Prayer in a boarding school outside High Wickham. Shirley and I were drawn together in the second round of the table-tennis tournament.

Thin as a rake, poignantly flat-chested, sinewy, imperious, athletic, dynamic, she bounced and swayed threateningly at the other end of the table, four or five bracelets rattling on each wrist, be-ringed fingers lifted to cover her laughter, long copper hair falling away from a cocked cheek. One of the Anglo Caths, I thought, even before she spoke. I had to sweat blood to beat her.

Perhaps it was the freedom and assurance she had which attracted me first, a strength of character and cheerfulness that meant you could never feel you were hurting her. And naturally I was impressed that someone from a higher class was interested in me. I liked the fact that her father was a lawyer, that the family was well-off, respectable, moneyed, and that my mother, with the way she always confuses respectability with morality, wholeheartedly approved of them. I was overwhelmed by all the contact of skin on skin, the way she shivered and melted when I kissed her ear, as I soon learnt to, the way she put a hand in my shirt as we walked across Gunnersbury Park. She liked to touch me. She wore a green silk scarf over her hair the way gipsies do, which somehow made me feel unspeakably tender, it gave her face such a bright, bird-like look, all eyes. But it was the sudden and complete intimacy that was most extraordinary. From the very first days together Shirley and I could talk about anything, everything. And amazingly we always agreed. She with me and I with her. It was uncanny. Had we not thrown religion and all its imponderables very promptly out of the window, we would have said we were made for each other.

So that on arrival back in Leicester that evening, I immediately turned to Shirley for support. Hadn't I been right? Hadn't I? One sounded mean saying certain things, but the fact was they had to be said. We talked it over. Shirley agreed wholeheartedly; it was a case, she decided, where the older generation, my mother, and the sixties aberration that had followed it, my sister, were both erring in sentimentality and romanticism, were refusing to look long and hard at future reality, future practicality.

Our room-mates Gregory and Jill were there, another solid sensible couple, and I was surprised, as we talked, how rapidly, on the basis of just a smattering of information, they came to the same conclusions I had. It was reassuring. Gregory said he found it extraordinary that people were even allowed to go on making the same old mistakes you read about in every novel, newspaper and social study, as if the centuries past had never been and the race had learnt absolutely nothing.

We cooked ourselves omelettes with green peppers and ate, unusually, in front of the TV, since BBC 2 was kindly interrupting the snooker to show somebody's version of *Carmen* (both Jill and Shirley came from the right class to be opera buffs). We drank some decent wine Gregory had tracked down that Sainsbury's had started importing from Friuli, and toasted to high-paying jobs and plenty of nights at the opera. 'But no running off with gipsy girls,' Jill frowned. 'Nor army boys,' Gregory replied.

We really were a happy foursome in that house. There were no overbearing characters, no martyrs, no one was even particularly idiosyncratic. We shared the housework and the bills. We studied quietly and helped each other. We all knew what we wanted and how to go about getting it. We were young, cheerful, optimistic.

In bed later that evening, Shirley said, 'Poor Peggy. Really.' And she said: 'Praise be to God for Reckitt & Colman though. A pink one a day keeps the gynaecologist away. Or the shotgun at bay. And you still can make hay. And have a damn good lay. Oh yea!' 'Oh shut up,' I laughed, trying as always to be serious. Though one of the best things about bed with Shirley was, not just the excitement, but the fact that this was when she was at her merriest. Sometimes we'd be reduced to such helpless laughter we'd have to give up and start all over again when we'd got over the giggles. 'Maybe,' she said, 'if Peggy's so anti hormone-juggling and all that, you could tell her to get a bedside book of jokes. Excellent contraceptive.' 'Just,' I said, 'that you'd always be worried she might miss the punchline.' 'She does seem,' Shirley agreed, 'a rather inattentive creature.'

Still, appreciating that sometimes I'm too quickly irascible and categorical, and because I really do love Mother and Peggy and wish them well, and since I felt I might yet influence the situation for the good somehow, I decided not to overreact and cut myself off from them. A few days after getting back to Leicester, I wrote Peggy the following letter:

Dear Peg,
      Sorry if I seemed like a bit of a bull in a china shop when I came down Tuesday. The fact is I'm really seriously worried about you and Mum, I mean about how you will cope if things start going wrong. Perhaps the best thing I can do is just list my fears, which I think you'll have to agree are not far fetched:

a) What if your actor man doesn't marry you and won't or can't support the baby?
b) What if you don't have enough money and have to go back to Gorst Road to bring him/her up amongst the mad and the senile?
c) What if Mother breaks down under the strain? Who will look after Grandfather and Mavis then?

Of course if either Mother or I or even yourself were well-off none of the above would be a problem, but even after I get out of university and hopefully get a job, it will be some years before I'll be able to spread any of the proceeds about, since Shirley and I will have to save for a home of our own. We can't rely entirely on her parents. My one thought is, and this is the last time I shall mention it, that it might be better to have an abortion now, get yourself safely married, save up a bit and then have the baby. That's all.

Hope you are well otherwise. Shirley and I are both gearing up for finals and making job applications. Fingers crossed.

All best, GEORGE.

She wrote back from an address in Holloway beside which she had scribbled the words: 'Temporary. Communicate via Mum.'

Georgie bruv – she wrote in blue wax crayon on a large sheet of graph paper – 'I might just as well ask, 1. What if a brick were to fall from a great height on your big head leaving you totally mentally handicapped? 2. What if Shirley's dad lost all his jolly lolly and you couldn't go horseriding at the weekends? 3. What if you were paralysed from the waist down in a hit-and-run accident and Shirley not only refused to push your wheelchair but ran off with a well-hung Rastafarian . . . ? See what I mean?

George, when you love a man as I love Dave, I mean love deeply, then you *want* to have a baby with him and he with you. It's something you both feel *in your souls*. It's the ultimate human experience. And once it's started, the baby I mean, you can't say, no, no, we'll have it in three years' time, for the simple reason, brother mine, that 'it' would be a different baby, wouldn't it, not the baby of our love now, but the baby of our love then.

I shall have that baby too when the time comes, okay? No need to worry about Mum either as she has Big G on her side.

By the way, is it okay if I crash a night at your place on the way back from the Loughborough festival?

Lots of love and thanks, no really, for your concern. PEG.

Fair enough, I thought, if she insisted on being romantic about it ('baby of our love now', indeed, as if it wasn't just any sperm meeting any egg). Time would tell how right I was.

In the event, however, this was not to be the case. For coming back from her roadying at the Loughborough Festival, Peggy crashed not at our place but about fifteen miles away shortly after leaving the M6. It happened around midnight on the pillion of a 500cc Honda behind a bloke called Marcus Robbins, a folk singer apparently. They hit a broken-down, unlit Mini-van stationary in an underpass. Marcus was killed instantly. Peggy suffered only mild concussion, but miscarried.

She was heartbroken. I sat by her hospital bed for hours upon hours while she did nothing but cry and squeeze my hands. Her chubby face was pale. Carelessly she let her big breasts show through her nightdress, the kind of thing you just can't help noticing even when you don't want to. She cried and I felt very close to her and gave up my last week of revision to be with her, shuttling back and forth on trains and buses. We talked about this and that, and for the first time we talked about our childhood at home – Mother, Grandfather, Mavis – as something definitely past and gone. We were adults. I remember her surprising me by saying she often thought of Mother as the Virgin Mary and Grandad as the Devil. I never think in these terms. People are who they are. Anyway, who did that make Mavis? Some possession case JC ought to hurry up and heal? And where was the man himself? Certainly not me.

At one point, laughing through her tears, Peggy said: 'You want to bet Mum will find some way of saying it was her fault.' I smiled. 'Poor baby,' she whispered. 'Poor little baby.' Her plump cheeks ran with tears. In a kind of daze she said, 'You know there'll never never be another baby the same. In all eternity. I was going to call her Elsa. Don't you think it's a nice name?'

Deep true lover Dave didn't show up once the whole week they kept her in, but I didn't mention this. Sensibility so often seems to entail not mentioning the most painfully pertinent. Peggy should have been counting her lucky stars.

I Do the Right Thing

Shirley and I on the other hand were truly in love. We were quite sure of it. We had been together four years now, formative years. We had grown into each other, made sacrifices for each other. For the last two years we had had our bank accounts in common, at my insistence, since I felt that as soon as you knew something was the right thing, the best course of action was to commit yourself at once. Some people fret and fritter their whole lives away, wondering whether to take this plunge or that. It inhibits them in every area, love, work, play. They sit for years caught uncomfortably on the prongs of their fences. But I was eager to get a move on.

I was ambitious. I wasn't sure in what direction, but I was eager to prove myself. Half I would have liked to travel, see places, have adventures, half I wanted to get right down to it and make money now in the city I'd grown up in, buy a car, buy a house, then a better car, a better house, eventually go into business, politics, who knows. Over those last four years, since adolescence, the world had gradually been transformed from my prison to my oyster. I felt ready to dive in, rather than merely desperate to get out. And understandably I associated this change and the euphoria that went with it with Shirley.

In any event, it seemed important to get marriage out of the way. Shirley was fun to be with. She was attractive. She had hazel eyes and a straight nose with a tiny sprinkling of freckles (like a bouquet I told her) around the bridge. And we got on together. She was intelligent herself and she believed in me. She said I had a good mind, a good body, a good face, a good voice and rotten taste, but the latter, fortunately, she felt she could rectify. She smiled wrily. She had large, well-spaced, fine white teeth with just one small endearing chip on the left upper incisor – skiing accident, the Dolomites (whereas my own chip I owe to a scuffle in a playground on the Tubbs Road Estate). Her lips were wide, her manner, at least in social conversation, exquisitely sardonic and 'collected' I think must be the right word. She would never embarrass you. She was always cool, polished. And talented too. She could dance, play the piano, play tennis (all the upper middle-class accomplishments denied to Peggy and me. She could sing counterpoint alto to my solid harmony church tenor. We often, hamming it up, sang hymns and even anthems together about the house. Plus she was an eager lover and she swore blind she didn't want kids. Who wouldn't have married her?

Her parents lashed out on the clothes and rings. My mother, delighted, spent more than she need have done buying a Moulinex she would never have dreamt of getting for herself. The venue was Christ Church, Turnham Green. Peggy, Grandfather and Mavis were all there, Grandfather with his navy medals, Peggy in a whorish pink jumpsuit, but I shut my mind to any embarrassment, they couldn't harm me now. I had escaped.

In a lemon dress, hair permed for the first time in lovely copper ringlets, opals in her ears, wide eyes truly glowing as it seemed to me only hers could, Shirley whispered at the chancel steps: 'If only I had a pair of tits, I'd make quite a picture, *n'est-ce-pas?*'

For my own part, acknowledging stout Mr Harcourt's complacent approving, just very slightly boss-eyed smile, bespeaking wealth, respectability, unassailable common sense, I knew I had done the right thing. I was set. Why shouldn't we be happy?

We rented a flat in North Finchley and got down to business with the rat race. House prices were spiralling and we would have to spiral after them. Shirley quickly found a place teaching infants at a private school for girls, St Elizabeth's, a temporary arrangement as what she was really suited for was something in publishing or advertising maybe. But we both felt that this was a moment to swallow pride and get some experience behind us. We didn't want to live off her parents. Meanwhile I got a foothold on the bottom rung at InterAct Management Systems and proceeded to become an expert (perhaps I should say one of 'the' experts) in network planning. Within a couple of years I was turning out software they'd never dreamt of till I arrived.

There was Johnson, an electronics man retired young from the airforce having lost an arm; pompous, mannered, always a fresh handkerchief in his pocket and so on, but very sharp. He'd had the idea. Then there was a dithery, worried type, Will Peacock, a great adjuster of trouser belts and twister of ties. He was putting up the money he'd inherited, and at the time I arrived still losing it. To look at him, death pale, stooped and fiftyish at thirty-five, you'd have thought he'd been bleeding for weeks on end. He needed a transfusion. But these were the halcyon days of software design and really you couldn't go wrong (to my credit actually that I sensed this at once).

I remember the interview as one of the turning points of my life, one of those rare moments of real self discovery. These two dull three-piece men began to explain that they'd just won their first large contract, a network planning system for oil rig construction in the North Sea. The idea (it seems very old hat now) was that the constructors should feed into the computer all the information relative to task sequences and durations, specifications and quantities of material and labour required, estimated idle time, possibility or otherwise of simultaneous operation, etc. etc. and InterAct's custom-written network program would then schedule all their work for them, time their orders, give advance warning of when they would need to draw on specialised labour, programme their payments, spot liquidity problems way ahead, and so on. Any unforeseen hitch or delay (flash welders not available for three days, interest rates up half a per cent) and the project manager need only tap in the details on a portable keyboard to have complete rescheduling and costing of absolutely everything.

It caught my imagination, I suppose because of the wonderful vision of life it implied (I still love network planning). All the complexities of people working together, people with different skills and temperaments, from different races and social classes, all the complications of fashioning and fitting together a vast range of heterogeneous and often obstinate materials, the hazards of shifting massive structures tens of miles across lashing seas and anchoring them to the sludge or rock of the sea bed – all this was to be controlled by one man tapping rapidly on a portable keyboard. And any snag, obstacle, inconvenience, rather than being allowed to send the whole house of cards tumbling to the ground, would simply be absorbed, analysed, and then the entire structure very finely altered, re-tuned, counterbalanced, and set on its way again, all embarrassments and dilemmas foreseen and neutralised, all interpersonal relations and moral issues rendered superfluous, nothing left to chance. It seemed a worthy cause to me and obviously profitable.

I told them I was their man. I really was. I'd study night and day to get into it. I'd be an expert on network planning before the year was out (and it was already September). They could pay me the absolute minimum salary for the first six months and then we could negotiate something reasonable on the basis of my performance, but I really wanted this job. I gave full reign to my enthusiasm, and you've got to remember these were still the bad old days pre-Thatcher when enthusiasm, at least for work, was taboo. But instinctively, and the feeling was overwhelming, I knew I was doing the right thing. It's something I've noticed so often since then, that when I'm outside the exhausting claustrophobia of family and intimate relationships, my personality flowers, I get so damn confident. I knew I didn't have quite the qualifications they wanted, I knew less than zero about network planning, so rather than bluffing it I simply offered to come in at a low price and work my bum off. I was dealing with a couple of canny older guys who needed a bargain and, as I suspected, would know one when they saw it. 'Look, don't even bother interviewing anybody else,' I said with a sniff of humour so as not to sound unpleasant. 'Take me. Please. I can guarantee it won't be a mistake.'

In the end they picked up my soul for just £3500 a year. But I was sure I was the winner.

Perfectly Normal
Behaviour

In those days InterAct had its offices on the North Circ, just past the Pantiles Pub, on the right heading south. So coming out of the interview victorious and immensely pleased with myself, I took a bus down to Park Royal to tell Mum. She was praying with a young girl who had leukaemia. I got this info from Mavis who was watching the kind of television they will put on in the no-man's-land between breakfast and lunch. A diagram was showing how nuclear waste is sealed in canisters, a matter of burning concern for Mavis, who, one felt, could only have improved with a little radiation.

I waited for Mum, mooching about the poky old sitting room, savouring a feeling of detachment and maturity, examining here and there the pathetic objects that had inhabited my childhood, the Wedgewood, the quaintsy Hummels.

Finally Mother came downstairs with her dying girl. She was a stunningly pretty little thing, in her mid teens I imagine, a perfect, frail, pressed lily of a face, though with a silk scarf tight about her head; to hide hair loss I quickly supposed. I smiled sympathetically, but having embraced my mother the girl hurried out without sparing a glance for the rest of us. It's something I've noticed frequently about the walking wounded. They don't really want to be seen by the rest of us at the Crawley household. They're embarrassed they've had to go looking for unorthodox help like this. All the stronger Mother's pull must be to get them past the ogre of Grandfather at the door.

Hardly noticing me, Mother flopped onto the sofa and rubbed her fingers in her eyes. She seemed exhausted. I announced that after a brilliant interview I'd got a really promising job. She took her fingers from her eyes, focused on me and beamed. 'Oh how wonderful, George. You must tell me all about it.'

'Let's go out to lunch,' I said, 'Just us two. Celebrate.'

'Oh, I couldn't do that, Dad and Mavis . . .'

'Oh come on, you can leave Grandad and Mavis for once.'

She stood up smiling, smoothed down her dress, little girlish, looked around her, saw the other two imprisoned in their perennial sloth, television, newspaper, never a useful item in their hands, never an interesting comment to make, doing nothing but sapping away at her marvellous energy. She looked at them. They didn't offer. They didn't say, 'Go ahead, Jenny dear.' She hesitated, then said: 'Oh well, perhaps I could fix them a couple of pork pies and a little egg salad. I think there are some salady things in the fridge. Hang on.'

I went into the kitchen and watched her working rapidly with plates, tomatoes, lettuce, boiled eggs. I noticed that there was something very different between the way she did these things and the way Shirley did them. Difficult to pin it down though. Unless it was simply that Mother lacked Shirley's style, the way she has of turning a plate into a picture. Mother tended to fumble. There were cuts on her fingers. A tomato came out not in slices but rough fruity chunks. She wiped her hands on a torn dishtowel (showing Beefeaters) and we set out.

Perhaps this lunch was the happiest moment I ever had with my mother. We ate in a Greek place on Acton High Street near the railway bridge. Not ideal but what do you want in Acton in the late seventies. She was pleased as a child to be treated, perhaps more pleased, since children always think everything is due to them. She said: 'I'm so very glad you've got what you wanted, George. It's so important not to be frustrated and cooped up in life.' 'Kind of business that's going to go like a bomb,' I said, 'with the way labour costs are shaping up right at the moment. People just have to be efficient.' She said: 'Oh, this is lovely,' and she beamed.

Coming back from paying, though, I caught her frowning.

'Don't worry, it wasn't that expensive,' I laughed. 'I've got the money,' for it would have been like her to have spoilt things fretting about how much cash I had. But she said she was thinking of that pretty young girl with leukaemia who was almost certainly going to die.

Then leaving the restaurant an odd thing happened. I opened the door for her and she stepped out directly and really rather carelessly into the path of an older, patently working-class man dashing for the bus with three or four Co-op carrier bags swinging wildly from his hands; one of the bags slammed into her leg and, half turning, the man stumbled and almost fell. 'Fuckin' idiot!' he screamed, scrambling on for the bus. 'Fuckin' idiot your-fuckin'-self,' I roared after him. 'Why don't you watch where you're fuckin'-well going?'

No sooner were these words out than I realised what a huge milestone this was. I had never sworn in front of my mother before.

Collecting herself, she said: 'There wasn't any need for that, George.' And after a few moments walking, she said quietly: 'I hope you don't use that language often. It's so horrible.' But the time had come; I said firmly: 'Mum, you live in a different world, okay? A different world, another planet. The planet Goodness. And maybe that's fine for you. But I live here and now. Okay? Everybody says that stuff, you know, everybody, it's even tame.' She said: 'Perhaps they do, I just hoped you wouldn't.' As of old, she had her grating, meek-shall-inherit-the-earth tone. But I had absolutely no intention of excusing myself as I might have done five years ago. The terms of our relationship had changed. I offered the treats. Very soon I would be offering the financial protection too. And she couldn't expect to criticise me about my language or any other perfectly normal behaviour.

Contemporary Civilisation

Those good years. I see myself bolting down my muesli, buttering my toast, showing variously-coloured season tickets to variously-coloured conductors, the 260, the 12, learning to leave the carcinogenic dregs at the bottom of tuppenny coffees at the office, staring and staring at the green Hew-Pack screen, exploring strings, sprites, double trip codes (my own invention), glancing up at the frenzied chase of polished metal on the North Circ, brushing lunchtime sandwich crumbs from the keyboard, studying on the bus on the way home (never a headache then), catching the nine o'clock news and the business programmes, studying and calculating away on my little IBM till midnight and gone, while Shirley maybe did the dishes, prepared lessons, read her art books, phoned friends, picked up the comedies she liked on the box. The neighbours across the hall invited us over for drinks sometimes, but we discouraged it; they were a sweet couple, Mark and Sylvia, both cheerful and very attractive physically, but hopelessly dumb. There was no future in it. You see that more or less immediately with some people. They felt they'd arrived in their two-bedroom Finchley flat, while we were only beginning our way up. No point in doing much more than waving to each other.

More willingly we went to parties, dances, when we got to hear of them. We still loved each other's company, still shone in groups and enjoyed making a show of our happy relationship. Shirley would come and sit on my lap. We would get involved in friendly little tussles. You could sense people watching, envying. We had that off to a T. Or occasionally she cooked the most beautiful meals from French recipes to surprise dinner guests: Jill and Gregory, now resident in Hornsey, both in commercial insurance; Peggy, pregnant again (I didn't even bother offering advice this time, you learn to recognise someone's destiny after a while); and just every now and then Shirley's younger brother Charles, one of your pink champagne lefties (Cambridge third in Philosophy) of uncertain sexual orientation and extraordinary belligerence; despite Daddy's huge salary he had somehow wangled himself a council flat off the Goldhawk Road, which he referred to as 'my pad' and rarely slept in.

So we had these little treats, the odd evening in company. But mainly our life was just the glorious, as yet unsoured routine: the busy days, bus and office, the Mars bars, lager, Rothmans and *Evening Standard*s, the steeply rising curve of my career, weekend purchases of consumer goods, Shirley's teaching, parents' evenings and school plays, on and on, day in day out, but brightly peppered with our always successful lovemaking, the pleasure at gloomy weekends of leafing through brochures to choose Mediterranean holidays we could now easily afford. Surely this was the good life, a triumph really of contemporary civilisation, busy young urban people, working hard, living well, faithful to each other, honest. It seemed that nothing was lacking. In my defence I think I can say that had it been allowed to go on this way, I would have been the last person to want to change anything.

Shortly after they took me up to eight grand, Mavis had a third shot at killing herself, and finally got it right: whole bottle of Disprin in the early hours and then the head in the oven for good measure. I felt a little sorry for my mother who would inevitably see this as another defeat and find cause to blame herself, but at the same time I couldn't help feeling relieved that at least this weight had been taken off her shoulders.

Inevitably I was called in to deal with the practical side, the funeral arrangements. The difficulty here was to persuade Mother to go for a reasonably priced coffin and skip the rose tree bit at the crem which would have eaten up three months of her pension and would anyway have had to be shared with two other 'cinderellas', as Shirley rather quaintly put it. Likewise, when the back door was rotting away, when the fridge was faulty (occasionally defrosting itself all over the lino), when the bathroom window could never be properly shut because the wood had swollen, what on earth was the point of a wreath of pinks for mad Mavis? I did my best.

The surprise at the cremation, though, was that Grandfather cried. He said nothing, but tears streamed from his pulpy old eyes. Sitting next to him I put an arm round his thick back to comfort him and found him trembling with emotion. Foreseeing his own funeral was the only way I could explain it, for it is indeed awesome when the coffin suddenly slides away through black curtains and you know you will see that face (however unloved) never again; doubly awesome I suppose when you expect to be providing the object lesson yourself in the not too distant future.

It rained for the event. Peggy came late, in the last stages of gestation, accompanied by a tall blonde boy who may or may not have been the father. On trying to engage him in conversation he turned out to be Czech and spoke only the most broken English. Bob/Raschid had been informed but didn't turn up, so that apart from the family there were only two rather mysterious spinster types in plastic macs who we eventually discovered were the other founder members of the Harrow branch of the Elvis Presley Fan Club. We let them take away the deceased's record collection, rather generously I thought, since you never know how much that kind of stuff might be worth these days. Mavis had had no life insurance so there was no windfall to give the event any cheer, and after desultory conversation over coffee and digestives at Gorst Road everybody took their umbrellas and themselves off home.

In the Scirocco (disc brakes all round, electric windows), Shirley rather unexpectedly said: 'I do feel sorry for your mother though.' And over Tandoori chicken later, because we really had to get out of the house to brighten up, she said: 'I wouldn't mind you know if she got your Grandfather into a home now and came to live with us. She's okay.'

'No room,' I explained promptly.

'We won't be where we are forever.'

I shook my head: 'He'll never go into a home. And so long as he's in Gorst Road she'll stay with him. Then you're always saying how impossibly pious she is. Think, you'd have to stop swearing about the house, you'd . . .'

'It wouldn't be the greatest of losses,' she said coolly. 'One grows out of swearing.'

Could she really be serious? When we had our lives so splendidly worked out already. 'We'd have to cut out the quickies any time we felt like it.' Had she thought about that?

'That's true, but I've always preferred the unabridged bedtime version myself.'

I stopped eating and looked at her, her long fine face, big, prominent eyes, the curve of character in her jaw, my good-looking if rather sinewy wife. 'Come on, come on, Shirley! She'd always be reproaching us for not having children, you know what she's like. Go forth and multiply, the Christian family, and so on.'

'She's never said a word about it to me,' Shirley said, 'in fact I've always thought her admirably sensitive on that point. My own mother's much worse.'

'But you can see the reproach in her eyes, for God's sake. She doesn't need to say anything. That's the whole point about my mother; she is a reproach in herself.'

Shirley smiled. 'Hasn't it ever occurred to you, that the hang-up might be yours rather than hers, I mean, you imagine her reproaching you for things you feel guilty of anyway. You've substituted her for your conscience, it helps you to ignore it. You think, it's her fault I'm feeling guilty, it's just my stupid mum.'

'Three cheers for psychoanalysis,' I said brightly, filling my mouth with some fierce sauce or other. 'Want to know what I dreamt last night?'

But Shirley said: 'Anyway, I'd really rather like to have a kid now actually. Why not? In fact that's partly what I was meaning to talk about. We could find a bigger place, have a baby and your mum could look after it while we were at work.'

Errors of Judgement

On reflection, one of the many errors of judgement I made with Shirley was mistaking class for intelligence, class and perhaps academic ability. They had seemed such rock-solid guarantees of personality at the time. I should have reflected: a) that any society, in its struggle to maintain the status quo, has a natural tendency to associate the manners of its ruling class with an above-average mental capacity, and; b) that girls often tend to be great and successful swots during their school years, get eight As at 'O' Level, or whatever the new equivalent is, but that this is no indication of true intelligence, which, on the contrary, only emerges through long-term behaviour patterns and real-life choices. I should also perhaps have reflected on the lightness, even flightness with which Shirley adopts and then drops and then perhaps readopts all sorts of opinions and points of view. One week she is pro-Israeli, the next pro-Arab, depending on who has committed the most recent atrocity; one week she will stop taking sugar because it's bad for her skin and the next she'll start taking it again because she needs to put on weight, she needs more energy. In short, Shirley is a person who neither has nor holds any truly deep-seated opinions, is capable of following no one particular policy. So that I should have seen that her sensible line on children (that they were too risky a business and that people who wanted good careers couldn't afford the time a baby required and deserved – opinions that more or less reflected my own) might turn out to be short-lived. Yes, I should have seen it and been ready for it. Except that we were only eighteen when we met and I was in love with her.

'You do appreciate,' I broached it carefully back home in

bed, 'that this is a complete reversal of what you were saying only a few weeks ago. You remember? When Greg and Jilly were over and you were talking about that Ian McEwan thing you'd read. About not having children while there's this nuclear threat. A complete reversal.'

'So what?' she said. 'Maybe I'm growing up.'

'But we went over this before and you promised. No kids.'

'But that was years ago.'

'Right. Of course it was. Those are precisely the kind of things you have to decide long range.' And remembering something Mother once said, I told her: 'If a person can't keep a promise then what on earth's the point of making one? The whole point about promises is that they bind you across time. Or no?'

Without a word she got up, pulled on her dressing gown and went into the living room to watch TV. I stayed put in bed listening to snippets of some film, sinister music, raised voices. I went over everything that had been said. I reflected that as usual I was right. The problem was that my exasperation, which was partly fear, made me too harsh. I came over as inhuman. Presentation problem.

I got up, found my own dressing gown and padded after her. Shirley was sitting on the sofa staring glumly at the television, a glass of Grand Marnier in her hands. She always likes to have snob drinks about the house. So do I for that matter. I was struck then, in that moment watching her before she noticed me, by the hollow angularity of her intent face in gloomy TV light, the slumped position of her body. She looked singularly unattractive. But I'm always careful not to be swayed by such momentary perceptions. I knew Shirley was a good-looking woman and I was determined that our marriage would work out.

I went and sat next to her.

'I'm sorry,' I said.

She didn't so much as turn to look at me.

'Come on, Shirl, I'm sorry, I was too harsh. I must sound like a real chauvinist arsehole sometimes. Forget it.'

When she still didn't turn, I got up and went back to bed.

A few minutes later she came back into the bedroom herself. She snapped on the light. Blinding me.

'Let's go out,' she said.

'What?'

'We can go down to the Torrington. There's dancing till two Tuesdays.'

'But I've got to go to work tomorrow.'

'Likewise.' And she said: 'Listen, Crawley, if we don't have kids it's so we can make the most of our freedom, right? Whereas all you do is work. Work, work, work. There must be something else in life.'

Out on the High Road she walked with an exaggerated girlish flounce. Suddenly she turned and grabbed me and kissed me hard, forcing our lips together, fingers twined behind my head. We were under an umbrella. 'You know you're turning into an old office fart, George,' she said brightly. 'Our life is one great suburban bore.' I kissed her back, trying to return her passion. 'Come on, put your hand on my arse,' she said, so I did. 'Squeeze,' she said, so I did. And at the Torrington we danced excitedly, with an excitement I hadn't felt for some time, rubbing thighs, necking, clinging tight, then went home and tackled the titbit, making quite a feast of it. Come the morning, the office, the green screen, and I was shattered.

So much for the aftermath of Aunt Mavis's funeral. One could hardly ignore the fact that some crucial balance had tipped. Something was wrong. Over the weeks and months that followed Shirley became moody, difficult, aggressive, while I was simply doing everything in my power to tip that balance back, to get back to the halcyon days before that conversation. With this in mind I brought home flowers and bottles of good wine in abundance, I cut out evening working as far as was possible for someone with my responsibilities and aspirations; I cut out the karate class I'd started going to for my back and which I was thoroughly enjoying and proving surprisingly good at. Instead I bought tickets for the opera and for orchestral concerts and ballets which I knew Shirley liked and which I myself didn't mind.

What else? I found a stable in Totteridge where we could ride Sunday mornings for an outrageous price and rub shoulders with other young professionals like ourselves. I encouraged dinner parties, trips and acquaintances, even when I wasn't really particularly keen, even when, for example, I had my mind on the huge new programmes we were troubleshooting for Brown Boveri. I tried to get her to take an interest in some large item we could feasibly buy, a new car for example, and I brought home brochures of Cavaliers, Orions, Giuliettas and the like. That usually cheers people up. But most of all I began to suggest that if she didn't find St Elizabeth's sufficiently challenging – and surely she had already stayed far longer than we ever intended – she should look elsewhere for a job, try for something in publishing again, or broadcasting. That had always been the plan after all. The problem as I saw it was that she wasn't fulfilled in her work. She was bored. I even suggested she might think about coming into InterAct in some capacity. I was in a position to swing that now. But Shirley said on the contrary that she had no intention whatsoever of changing her job. What did publishers do in the end, sat in offices like everybody else, thinking of the price of paper. No, she owed to St Elizabeth's the discovery that she had a vocation for small children. She loved her children. Really, she loved their eagerness, their innocence. In fact she loved teaching in general. It was fun. She had never expected she would, but there you were. She would be dead without her job. It was the only good thing in her life.

'So,' I said, mustering what enthusiasm I could, 'why not get into a whole load of extra-curricular activities? The plays and concerts they're always asking you to do. That could be exciting. Bury yourself in it, if you like it so much.'

'You are a love,' she said. 'Such a delight.'

One Tries and
Tries to be Sensitive

Another thing I had to put up with these days were the frequent visits from Shirley's mother.

Mrs Harcourt was a busy, bossy, bustling woman, exhibiting all the character traits of the wife who gives up career for family and is then left stranded when the fledgelings fly the nest (an object lesson for Shirley if only she'd had eyes to see it). She spent an inordinate amount of time on her personal appearance (hair-do's, sauna, massage), and had taken up photography as a hobby to fill in the becalmed oceans of time between one social function and the next. She always had her camera bag when she came to visit and at some point or other would always pull out a Nikon and take her glasses off to squint through its expensive auto-focusing lens at some unlikely subject, in fact the more unlikely the better, to show what an eye she had, how she saw 'the unusual in the usual', as she put it.

She squinted through the lens, maybe at a mess of saucepans inside one of our cluttered cupboards, maybe at soap suds being sucked into the drain, at a coffee mug balanced on the arm of the sofa, but as far as I remember she never clicked the shutter in our house and certainly never showed us any of the results if she did. Perhaps not even she could find anything sufficiently unusual, we are such regular people. She had put on two small shows at the local library in Chiswick, one depicting, from *de rigueur* unlikely angles, various stages of slaughter in a poultry abattoir off the Goldhawk Road, a comment on man's barbarity to the chicken apparently, the other featuring pieces of flotsam and jetsam washed up on the mudbanks opposite the family's Strand-on-the-Green house, clammy with slime and generally unrecognisable. The glaring gratuitousness of these enterprises was one of the few things Shirley and I were still capable of laughing about together.

Otherwise, Mrs Harcourt was a signed-up, card-carrying member of the newly formed SDP, as perhaps only an already wealthy unemployed person could afford to be. Her small head came surprisingly forward from her body and when she spoke, her crisp elocution set a fierce mole above one corner of her mouth in undulating motion. Perhaps this accounted for the immediate impression of pushiness she communicated.

She would come over in her Metro Deluxe, maybe three, four times a week, shortly after Shirley got back from school. When I arrived home a couple of hours later I wasn't invited to join in whatever discussion was under way. Often they sat together in the kitchen or even the bedroom to make it clear they wanted to be on their own. Once I heard crying. More often there were loud peals of haw-hawing women's laughter, Mrs Harcourt gasping for breath, probably holding her sides the way older women will, shrieks of 'Oh dear, oh dear', Shirley no doubt tossing her hair back, glistening pink mouth wide open, the gesture that had most enchanted me when first I met her.

'So what do you find to talk about?' I might ask later.

'Oh, this and that.'

'Come on, she's here every other evening. There must be something.'

'About Dad, about Charles. She's worried that he never seems to have any girlfriends. You know.'

'I'd be worried for the girl if he did.'

'Then he was arrested last week in some anti-Cruise march.'

'He likes to be arrested, it reinforces his council flat credentials.' And off the cuff I asked: 'What's the score with your dad these days anyway? We haven't seen him for donkeys.'

Shirley said: 'What a lemon this cooker is. For God's sake! You can never be sure what the temperature is. It doesn't matter how you set it. Either the stuff comes out like charcoal or everything's raw in the middle.'

'And me?' I asked with what I hoped was a wry smile.

'What?'

'Don't you talk about little old George?'

'Aren't we insecure?' she laughed. She said: 'Of course we talk about you sometimes. It'd be odd if we didn't. Wouldn't it?'

'Would it?'

'I think so.'

'Okay. And what do you say?'

'Oh, that you don't deserve me.' She stabbed a fork into some casserole meat and smiled sweetly.

'Tell me more.'

'Mmm, let me see, that your background's made you a repressed hypocrite.'

'Ah, of course, that. Examples?'

'Though naturally we always agree that deep down you're a kind, honest man and you'll probably turn out good in the end.'

'Naturally.'

But I think I can tell a knife when it's out. And turning.

I suggested that we try to get away more often if she felt so down. An occasional weekend in Paris; we could afford it now. We were averagely well-off young people, even if we might have done better to save. Or I could even take a week off at Easter. Maybe we could go to Spain, Italy. Or a few days riding somewhere. She said she didn't want to go away for a weekend, let alone for Easter. She didn't even want to go away in the summer. We were planning to drive down to Turkey that year, seeing as everybody else seemed to be going to Greece. Now she didn't want to go. I could go on my own. I said, no, I could not go on my own. What was the point? 'Why not?' she said. 'In your head you live entirely on your own all the time.'

One tries and tries to be sensitive. I said that if she felt really depressed and unhappy maybe, just maybe, she should see somebody, er, get help, I don't know, a psychoanalyst or something. She said: 'Do me a favour, sweetheart, please.' And she said: 'This flat is impossible, really impossible, you know that? Not a single window that gets the sun, the carpets are the worst dust traps imaginable, the drains stink, the cupboard doors don't close, the hot water's never hot enough, the pipes groan, the oven's useless, the paint is nearly grey, and you can never do anything about it because the landlady doesn't want to pay for it. I mean, what are we doing here?'

I felt she was rather exaggerating. Still, at least this was something I could deal with. I suggested that if it was the flat that was depressing her, though she could never say I didn't help with the cleaning and so on, then why didn't we buy our own place now instead of waiting.

'With whose money?' She was aggressive. I said she knew perfectly well with whose money. A bit of our own and a great deal of her father's. Surely it was tacitly understood that when we were ready, he'd help us to buy. She said buying our flat wouldn't solve anything. The flat was awful, but it wasn't that that was getting her down. I said I didn't know what else to suggest, it seemed to be me making all the suggestions and then her promptly telling me I was stupid every time I opened my mouth. I couldn't understand why we couldn't be happy.

'Don't suggest anything,' she said. 'And above all, stop buying me flowers as if I were dying or something.'

Carrying the Gloomy Can

My mother came over. I think for my birthday. Mother is a great celebrator of birthdays, even when everybody else has forgotten them. She even remembers Hilary's. It's a ritual for her, a slavery almost, like the moral code she blindly follows, the tithe of her income in the collection plate, the sense of duty toward Grandfather, the not marrying a man because he'd got divorced a decade before.

She remembered my birthday and brought the traditional, home-baked, lemon-iced birthday cake, arriving at the door after two long bus rides all bright and chirrupy, because of course Mother is never more cheerful than when she knows she's fulfilling some family duty. I thanked her and kissed her. I was even glad she'd come as I felt it might take some of the tension out of the air. But hardly have we sat down to eat our cake than Shirley is asking: 'Saved any souls lately, Mrs Crawley?'

It was deliberately hurtful. She had the innocent smile on her face she always combines with her worst sarcasm. My Mother very simply said: 'It's not me saves souls, lovey, it's God,' and she began to tell us all about Peggy's darling little boy Frederick. He was so big and blond, he had all his milk teeth already, he was such a gorgeous cuddly little boy. Her big clumsy hands massacred the cake with the flat's blunt breadknife. 'For you, George?'

Shirley asked: 'I imagine Peg's planning another one now?'

Naturally, given the still dubious paternity of the first, this had Mother knitting her brow. But she managed a forgiving laugh: 'Oh, I wouldn't know, Peggy never tells me anything.'

'Vetting possible fathers, perhaps,' Shirley suggested. 'She's into Buddhism these days, isn't she? Perhaps we'll have a Chinese in the family.'

When we were on our own a moment in the kitchen I asked her what the hell she thought she was up to. Why couldn't we just have a pleasant meal together?

'I hate,' she said, 'the way you're such a goody goody when your mother comes, the way she thinks the sun shines out of your backside. If she knew what you were really like.'

'And what am I like?' I asked.

'You hardly need me to tell you that,' she said.

'You were the one, sweetheart,' I told her, 'said you wouldn't mind her coming to live here with us.'

'Precisely because,' she replied, 'she might finally be forced to see the light. We might clear the air.'

'I swear in front of her,' I said, 'I don't try to hide anything.'

At which, and I'm afraid this is very effective, she simply burst out laughing and walked back into the living room.

Driving Mother home to Acton, I said: 'Sorry if Shirl was a bit abrasive, Mum.'

'Was she, love? I didn't notice.'

'I don't know, she seems a bit, er, frustrated these days. I don't know what it is.'

'We all go through our bad patches, poor dear,' Mother said complacently. Then waiting for the lights at the A40, she hazarded: 'I know it's none of my business, but perhaps it's time to start a family. She did tell me she'd like a baby a while back.'

When I said nothing, watching for green – I had the usual hassler trying to edge past me on the inside, something I never allow – she said: 'I always feel there's a time in everybody's lives when it's just the next logical step to take, the only way to grow.'

I laughed, putting my foot down hard. I love driving. I said, 'You forget, Mum. I specialise in logical steps, it's my job, and I can assure you it wouldn't be. Shirley's is just a straightforward case of boredom. That's the problem. Have a baby and she'd be even more bored. She'd always be trying to dump it on babysitters and relatives.'

Mother said brightly: 'Well you know you can count on me, love. I have ever so much fun looking after Frederick.'

With a sense that events were in danger of getting beyond my control, I rang up Shirley's father the following week and began a very, but very careful spiel I'd prepared in every detail: about Shirley being depressed because of the miserable flat we'd been in too long, about the landlady never wanting to decorate or replace anything, about the rental market being so hopeless these days with the ludicrously pro-tenant rules the Labour government had introduced and Margaret hadn't as yet got round to repealing, about the price of property being so high it was unimaginable for two young people to buy a decent place on their own – and I asked him was there any chance, now I'd put a bit of money together myself, because I was saving about thirty per cent of my income – was there any chance that he could maybe chip in, rather massively actually, and . . .

He said: 'Not till I'm sure just how the settlement's going to go with Mary, I'm afraid.'

It was lunchtime and when I'd got the phone down I looked at the world map on the wall where tiny flags showed all the countries where my software was being used. From Panama to Portugal, it said on the brochure, Austria to Australia. Why is it, I wondered, that I am always to be excluded from the intimate affairs of the lives of people close to me? Why? Why do they keep me out? I was hurt, angry.

'But why should you need to be told?' Shirley retorted.

'Because we're married for Christ's sake! Because we're supposed to be sharing our lives. You complain I don't understand you and then you don't tell me what I need to know to have a chance. Obviously it's been upsetting you. It explains everything. And I've been faffing about in the dark for months.'

She said perhaps I was right. Yes, probably I was right. But she just hadn't felt like telling me. She hadn't the heart to talk about it. It was so awful. Her parents had been such a fixed point in her life, she'd never even realised really.

She was on the brink of tears, and for once I was allowed to console her.

But over the next months, though it seemed impossible, and above all unnecessary, the tension heightened. Shirley would be sullen and moody on my arrival home and almost anything I said would cause a flare up. I might innocently ask what was for dinner and abruptly be told I could bloody well get my dinner myself. I might, despite office weariness, traffic weariness, a briefcase full of work, offer to go to the Indian shop, pick up some goodies, and immediately have to hear that since I was no good at doing the shopping and always brought home the wrong things there was no point in my going, was there?

Of course, from what one gathers from magazine articles, TV documentaries, radio plays while washing the car, etc., it did occur to me that Shirl might be suffering from some sort of physical/mental illness, or even stress, and that perhaps I should be feeling sorry for her, rather than the opposite. This I honestly tried to do. But then I also thought that if she was prone to suffering from, say, clinical depression (though she never had so suffered in the seven previous years I'd known her), then I personally didn't want to be the one who carried the gloomy can for the rest of my life, did I? It was a serious problem.

I stroked the wispy hair at the fine nape of her neck as she sat on the floor, back to the sofa, watching TV. She shook my hand off.

Or at least scenes like this occurred. Why couldn't we be cheerful?

I said: 'Fancy a pint down the Torrington? Bound to meet somebody.'

She didn't reply.

'Bit of a tipple, pinch your nipple.'

Nothing. No response.

I phoned her brother Charles, met him in a pub in Kentish Town and over a couple of jars asked him what he thought.

Had Shirley ever suffered from depression as a child? He smoked heavily from my pack of Rothmans, playing a fifty-p piece across pale knuckles. He said Shirley had always been the parents' favourite, they had always given her everything – ponies, dance classes, skiing holidays – while he had largely been ignored and then generally made fun of when he tried to point out the social injustice their lifestyle implied. He had given the Filipino maid a wad of notes from Father's wallet once, though, intimidated and conditioned as the girl was, she had handed them straight back to Mother, after which his father had given him a thorough beating. That was the kind of family it had been. The difference being that while he rebelled, Shirley had lapped it up, and what she was reaping now was precisely the fruit of her mindless and selfish upbringing, the *ennui* of the directionless bourgeoisie. She needed a cause, a sense of purpose. He himself was on a local committee which tried to ensure that eligible people got rehoused. He had been instrumental in saving a number of squats which had been under threat from eviction. He was never depressed at all. With all the suffering there was in the world, he said, it was so damn obvious what one should do with one's life that he couldn't understand people lounging around moping.

It didn't seem worthwhile arguing with someone whose views were so far beyond the pale, so I drank up, paid and got out. Though that evening, just for the record, as it were, I did suggest to Shirley that she might get involved in one of those groups that provides free crèches for working-class mothers.

'Please,' she said, chopping lemon, 'are you out of your mind? Or do you want to turn me into your mother or something?'

So finally I put it to her. Could it really all be simply because she wanted a child?

Could all what be?

Her being so depressed and unfriendly (not to mention obtuse).

'Oh that. Just a phase,' she said, breezing about with

saucepans. She kissed me on the side of the neck as I tucked into chops.

'So it's not that you want a baby?' I often do wish, with Shirley, that I had my dictaphone in my pocket.

She shook her head rather exaggeratedly, refusing to take me seriously. I was patient.

'No, because I mean if it is that, I mean, if you really want children,' I took a deep breath, 'then seeing as I don't, I don't know why, but I really don't, I feel complete and happy without them, then I think the best thing to do would be for us to split up so that you'll be in plenty of time to find another man and we can stop making life a misery for each other. Which seems a crime frankly. I mean,' I hurried on, talking at her back now as she sloshed water in the pans – Shirley always seems to be doing something with pans – 'I personally don't want us to split up, at all, I really don't, I just want us to be happy together. I've said it a thousand times. However, if you . . .'

The saucepans are the new, slow cooking, heavy metal kind, and cost a good month's salary. Though I'll give her they're stylish. I never objected to such purchases. On the contrary, I encouraged anything that would make her happy. I was always so relieved when there was something she actually wanted.

But now at last she turned. She stood with her backside hitched up against the draining board, her fingers gripped to its edge. She was wearing glossy blue running shorts. She looked at me and looked at me and at last after all these months she burst into tears. She wept and suddenly crouched down over pitted red-and-black chequered lino. She said of course she didn't want us to split up. How could I even imagine such a thing? And she was sorry if she was being unpleasant and bloody-minded. She didn't even know why she was like this herself. But she felt so upset about so many things. Honestly. And she burst into tears again.

Tears, I must say, have a quite overwhelming, even disabling effect on me. I have never been able to resist them. I had been unable to resist my mother's as a child and I was unable to resist Shirley's now. Hence at this point I gave up any attempt to follow the argument through to some sensible conclusion and hurried from the table to go and comfort her. We cuddled, she cried, I whispered softly, we kissed, looked into each other's red eyes, confessed, forgave, kissed again and eventually, arriving somehow in the bedroom, made love, with me foolishly, if not unnaturally, hoping the tide had turned.

There followed a very happy two weeks of perfect reconciliation, relaxation, fun. So, yes, it was still possible. Everything was hunky-dory. Turkey was on. We bought our ferry tickets, got the car serviced. We were going to have a great time. Life was great. And then it began all over again: arguments, sulking, general bitchiness. Turkey off. Not only Turkey, but any other holidays I might be planning too. Okay? When I reminded her of all she'd said that evening, all she'd conceded, she either refused to acknowledge that such a scene had ever taken place, or she'd try some bright sardonic line like: 'All under duress, Your Honour, under duress. My lawyer wasn't present. I retract everything.' Or she'd throw back her head, laughing, and say, 'Oh George, I do love the way you always, always believe you're right. You're a phenomenon.'

I spoke to no one about this. Every morning I went into work, joked with Tony, my assistant programmer, flirted mildly with the secretaries, Joyce and Sandra, reported to Johnson and Will Peacock, wined and dined clients, made rude jokey propositions down the phone to switchboard. No doubt you can picture it, the average stale-tobacco, fluorescent-lit office life, with all the little formalities and pleasantries and gallantries, the way you live and brush up against people and talk behind each others' backs and generally get on famously.

I spoke to no one. Probably it was the same for Shirley. Jolly and lively at work, glum and offhand at home. As if we were only our real selves of old when we arrived in the safe environment of the office, the school. If other people came, Mark and Sylvia, determined to be neighbourly (had we noticed the lock didn't engage on the front door, and what about the state of the lawn?), forcing their way in with a few cans of Whitbread's or a tin of chewy flapjacks, we put on a great front. Shirley was almost too dazzling, I drank heavily, but as soon as they were gone, we slumped. The television. A newspaper. Separate bedtimes.

And it was on one of these evenings, as I remember it, that my heart hardened. I use that Biblical expression because at last after a childhood of Bible studies I understood what it meant: a deliberate, quite conscious shutting oneself off from the tenderer emotions. My heart hardened. I'd had enough.

This is What I Should Have Gone For

Grandfather had become entirely incontinent. I had my suspicions frankly that the old NHS had rather cocked up the prostectomy, maybe whipped out something they shouldn't have, bit of sphincter or something, but as Shirley said, you'd never get to the bottom of it. Nor was Grandfather likely to generate much sympathy in tabloid newspapers or even a court of law were one to try for some compensation. Instinctively people would see he deserved it. So I spent a little time every morning checking out the geriatric home situation. I gave exactly fifteen minutes, ten thirty to ten forty-five, to phoning up all the various bodies concerned. I felt in this way I'd be informed and prepared when the crunch came and wouldn't have to lose a whole week finding out the score right at some critical moment when I had a new project on my hands or something.

The problem, my enquiries revealed, was that the old man wasn't suffering from senile dementia. Had he been suffering from senile dementia and hence truly in danger of doing damage to himself, accidentally putting the electric kettle on the gas, or setting his jacket on fire when lighting his pipe, then they would have taken him in (though with something like that on the cards one couldn't help feeling it might have been worth hanging on to him for a while). Otherwise, they encouraged home care, and given that the social worker had reported my mother as being 'valiant and willing, if a little overprotective', they were of the opinion he should remain in Gorst Road.

Well, with property prices rising sharply again, I felt on reflection that this solution suited me for the moment too.

Hang on a few years, then get a whole bundle of money for the house, enough not just to pay for Grandfather's home but to leave something to spare for setting up Mother in a small place of her own as well. That way we wouldn't be forced to take her in ourselves.

Until two things happened in the same week. Grandfather fell down the stairs and bust his hip, and Mother, who now had to wash him and change him like a baby at all hours of the day and night, came down with some sort of virus that completely floored her. She phoned me feebly at 7 a.m., having waited of course until the third day of this illness before 'bothering me'.

I drove over in excruciating traffic to the banana republic of Hackney, aiming to winkle out the ever phoneless Peggy and take her over to Park Royal to help out. In the event, however, the gipsy painted third-floor door of her bedsit was answered, not by my sister, but by a rather stout Indian woman, the kind with a beachball of brown belly showing through gaudy drapes and a neat red bullet-hole in her forehead. She was holding the lardy and wriggling young Frederick, while her own (presumably) two small girls peeped duskily from behind her sari – beyond which, a backdrop of carelessness and charity-shop makeshift. I noticed a saucepan on the carpet, for example, a newspaper torn to shreds.

Peggy had a job, the woman said. Where, doing what, how could I get there? She didn't know. Which again is typical of Peggy. She gets a babysitter and then doesn't bother to explain how she can be contacted. What was the woman supposed to do if the child fell ill, if there was an emergency? But Peggy always imagines all will go well. This was what she had taken over from our childhood religion I suppose: faith. Well may it serve her. Still it was good to think there was another income in the family.

I drove over to Gorst Road, another hour simply tossed into the maw of the capital's time-gobbling traffic system, and had to wait a further five minutes for Mother to drag herself down to the front door, since I'd forgotten my own keys. She was quite ashen and complaining, very unusually for her, of crippling stomach pains. Had she seen a doctor? No she hadn't and didn't want to. It was just a bug. But she must go and see her doctor. For heaven's sake! She wouldn't. But . . . She wouldn't. She hated doctors. God would take her in his own good time. My mother actually said that. I hugged her all the same and half carried her in her nightie to the sofa; then went up to see Grandfather; the stink on the landing, however, told me more than I needed to know and I went back downstairs.

Mother had now stretched out on the couch. 'I'm sorry,' she whispered. 'And the social services, for Grandfather, have you been in touch?' Apparently a social worker would come in the next couple of days. 'So we should take him to hospital. Immediately. Where they can look after him.' But he didn't want to go to hospital, she said. He refused. He'd shout and scream if you tried. 'I'm sorry,' she said again. She closed her eyes and sighed, holding her stomach. I thought: 'Incredibly, these two people are my responsibility. This is my family. And I'm supposed to be meeting my contact from Tektronics for an early lunch.' I asked: 'Isn't there anybody from the church could help?' She shook her head. There was, but they were on holiday.

For a moment I stood helpless in the dark cave of my childhood sitting room, trapped again: the photographs, the Wedgewood, the dusty naïveté of the Hummels, the sullen rhododendrons outside the window, and, blending it all together, an all-pervading sense, which was also a smell, of brown. Somehow the place stank of brown. There I stood. Until the obvious occurred. There is nothing you can't pay your way out of. And even though it was going to be expensive, I moved to the phone.

That evening I finished work as early as I could and drove to Gorst Road for about seven to check that all was well and we were getting our money's worth. The nurse was tall and pleasantly bulky, her hair done up in a bun on a long thick neck, one of those women who carry weight well, moving about with a crisp rustle of uniform and tights faintly chafing together between strong legs. In her early thirties, I guessed, efficient, assured, getting through. 'Will do, Mr Crawley,' she said in response to some request or other, and I told her to call me George.

Upstairs I found Mother asleep in her green nylon sheets (Shirley would wince just at the thought) and the passageway beyond now smelling almost sweetly. I looked in on Grandfather to find him sitting up with the *Express*. Every piece of clothing, towel, dressing-gown, string vest, was neatly, femininely folded. Even the old man's still black, rather fierce hair was combed flat, his cheeks shaved. He looked surprisingly virile, as if he might spring up into action at any moment. I smiled. 'Had to get a nurse in,' I said. 'Bit expensivo, but there you go.' He looked at me quizzically. 'Good day at the office?'

I thought of the nurse talcing his loose old balls and bum. I thought, if only one could afford the service on a regular basis, family life could be made quite pleasant. In our own case, as long as it wasn't for more than two or three nights, it would be worth every penny. And on the way downstairs, noting how the threadbare patches were bigger now, the bannister rail looser, it occurred to me that I might have sex with this nurse. Why not? I could tell Shirley I had to stay the night with Mother and I could perhaps get a leg over in mine and Peggy's old room. That should exorcise a few ghosts.

Her name was Rosemary. I went out and bought stuff for her to prepare herself some dinner (thanks to Shirley I am actually quite an astute shopper) and we ate together over fantasy Formica in the kitchen and talked. It was really most pleasant, Rosemary's company, a quite unexpected treat. I felt so easy, so relaxed, I amazed myself. Especially since I had been wondering recently whether I didn't need tranquillisers. She explained, when I marvelled at all the little extras she'd done, that nursing wasn't her vocation at all, she had wanted to be a pianist. She had trained and trained and very nearly made it, but not quite. Then not having quite got married either, she had decided she must have a safe source of income.

She had taken up nursing, but signed on with an agency, rather than staying with the NHS, 'to be flexible', she said. Now she quite liked the job in a curious sort of way. My grandfather, for example, had been terribly sweet, had told her all kinds of interesting stories.

I didn't object. I listened, and listening, supping whatever cans I'd found in the local subcontinent emporium, I remember being delighted by the straightforwardness of all this, another life unfolding so sensibly, so poignantly; and as so often when I meet a new woman, regardless of looks, I realised that this was the woman I should have married: cheerful, practical, generous, talented, not overly bitter about her disappointments, getting on. She had large white sensible teeth, long pale fleshy hands that seemed to have a quick active almost animal life of their own. There was something nervously vibrant about them as they lay still on the tablecloth, like starfish almost, damp, soft, alive. No nail varnish. No frills. This is what I should have gone for.

After eating, she asked permission, lit up a cigarette and then, for no reason I could see, simply smiled directly at me. Her lips, which weren't well defined, had a rather sad wise twist, blowing out smoke. Her cheeks were full. And I recalled something I'd been thinking lately, on a bus somewhere, watching somebody kiss somebody: that all young women, however apparently plain or even ugly at first glance, all have their little attractions, their charms, their lures, not one without some way of catching your eye: a ready smile of complicity, a way of cocking the head so that hair falls to one side (why does this attract me so much?), a way of lightly touching your wrist perhaps, or of taking a knuckle in the mouth to laugh. One way or another, and consciously really I often think, they compensate for what they may not have, that archetypal body. So with Rosemary, her frank friendliness, utterly without flirtation, her acceptance of you, without any of the barriers of male-female social manoeuvring (*viz* Joyce, the more unnattainable the gigglier and flirtier she became), all this seemed to draw attention to the large fleshy presence of her body as something straightforward, animal, loveable, that might well embrace you, without difficulty, without anxiety, if only it could be unlocked from that angular uniform.

Her breasts were inescapably large, even extravagant.

And I was just getting definite ideas into my head, toying with breathtaking strategies, thinking it would be wise to drink a bit more for courage, when Peggy arrived, complete with baby Frederick and, after rushing up to see Mother, announced (she had cropped her hair since last I saw her) that she would be staying the night in her own room. So that in the event I was left with the rather less voluptuous, though not entirely unsatisfactory curves of the North Circular.

Wild Summer Rain

I don't know what took hold of me that night. I went to bed, as usual, an hour or so after Shirley, having read, perfectly calmly, through a couple of hardware reviews I like to keep up with. I undressed and slipped under the quilt. It was July, but raining hard outside. In just two weeks we were supposed to be going to Turkey, except that all was up in the air with Shirley's saying she didn't want to come. Would I go on my own? Hardly. But the place on the ferry was booked. Why couldn't Shirley be more reasonable?

Almost at once I realised I wasn't going to sleep. I lay still. I assumed my customary sleeping position. No chance. I was in a state of such extreme physical and mental alertness. My skin seemed to sing and crawl with contradictions. There was just so much blood in me, unused, unfulfilled. I clenched my fists, my toes. I ground my teeth. For a while I surrendered to the most vivid erotic images, my tongue pressed against the blue cotton swell of a girl's plump panties, for example, that sort of stuff. Then trying to force my mind elsewhere, I wondered about my mother's life, its astonishing sexless serenity. How could people be so different from each other? What had happened to the straightforward sensible life I had planned?

Zombie-like, as if controlled from elsewhere, I sat up in the stale dark half light. I stood and went to the window, immensely tense, aware of sweat on my hands. Pushing back the curtain revealed the inevitable parallel lines of stationary cars, gleaming dully in rain and lamplight down to the dripping park. 'My whole life,' I thought, recalling Charles, while at the same time reflecting how unlike me this was, 'has been nothing but a pathetic trundling along on the metalled rails of my early social and sexual conditioning.' Confused, excited, I pulled some clothes on, found my shoes.

For more than an hour then, without an umbrella, wearing nothing more than Terylene trousers and a cotton shirt, I walked the respectable brick streets of Finchley. I sucked in the fresh damp air. I felt at once bursting, bursting with strenuous life, and at the same time paralysed, trapped, marching at a zombie-ish pace. But trapped by what? Was anything or anyone preventing me from doing as I chose?

I walked. The wild summer rain fell in dark gusts and clattered against sensible silent houses, the black gloss of blind suburban windows. And so I began to plan very definitely how I would invite Rosemary on holiday to Turkey in place of Shirley. Why should she say no? I would pay for everything. She had taken up agency nursing to be flexible, she said. She wasn't married, she said.

I planned my approach in immense and teeth-gritting detail. I would have nerves of steel. I would say this, say that, smile that smile which Shirley had told me was sexy. And I fantasised what would follow, hot nights in Turkish hotels, Karma Sutra positions followed by good cheerful meals in spicy restaurants. Other people found relief in affairs, didn't they? I had even heard a somewhat embarrassing and wimpy confession from Gregory recently.

I didn't sleep at all that night. I sat in the living room reading through papers from work, and the following morning, bewilderingly early, a good half an hour before she was due to be substituted, I was pushing into Gorst Road from a breezy damp morning to put it to Rosemary. Turn the key, customary tug and push, and the door was open.

'Hello, love,' Mother's voice sang, 'I'm back on my feet.' Embracing me, she said, 'It's something of a miracle really. I felt so ill yesterday.'

Indeed she still looked frail as rice paper. Though she gave a little clap of her hands and beamed. Which is a way she has. Rather as if we were at Sunday school, singing choruses.

'And the nurse?'

'I sent her home, poor dear, she was so tired. I think I can cope myself now. To be honest she was being rather bossy with poor Dad. I'm just making tea for Peggy if you want a cup.'

Peggy was still in bed, despite the fact that her infant could be heard yelling in the kitchen.

I suppose it must be indicative of the state I had got myself into, or rather that Shirley, that life had got me into, that only two hours later, as soon, that is, as I had a moment alone in the office, I was actually on the phone to this girl I had merely eaten a frugal meal with, watching her slow white hands as she fed herself.

'I got your number from the agency. I said you'd left your purse.' 'Oh did I? How silly of me. I'll . . .' 'No, no you didn't.' 'What?' 'You didn't leave it. I got your number because I want to see you again. I enjoyed meeting you so much.'

After a short pause, she said: 'You do realise you just woke me up. I've been on my feet all night.'

'I'm sorry,' I said. I was ready to hang up the moment she said no. I truly did like her but I couldn't see myself hanging on the phone and begging. My wife was a misery was the point. I wanted some fun.

She said: 'Okay, how about next Friday?'

I put the phone down and stared around me: the desk, the Venetian blinds, the attractive HewPack hardware. Done it! Done it!

If you really want to do it, George. If you really want to be that person.

I stared, pushing the knuckles of both hands together, biting the inside of a cheek, concentrating. And realised I hadn't really thought this through yet. I hadn't decided. My heart wasn't that hard. The truth being, I suppose, that for some people – Peggy springs to mind – new departures of this kind are just water off a duck's back; experience doesn't touch them deeply whatever they do, and so any course of action is more or less as good as the next. While for others of us, for me, it is a bath of acid. Did I really want to become an adulterer? There was a fear of changing, of losing myself somehow, a fear my mother had always exploited. I would far rather be good and stay put, if only one could have fun and pleasure with it.

Why couldn't Shirley be pleasant?

By six o'clock that evening I had spent so much time blind in front of my screen agonising and wrangling with myself – Rosemary yes, Rosemary no (and how was I to explain my Friday evening outing?) – that I came to the conclusion that I must, must force the decision at once, tonight, or go mad and quite possibly lose my job into the bargain.

When I arrived home, Shirley had just come out of a long session with her mother who was now quite blatantly using her daughter as a recipient for all the bitter things she had to say about her father. Not something likely to improve our own marriage. The moment Mrs Harcourt was out the door I told Shirley I wanted to have a serious talk with her. She said, with her usual blithe irony, to fire away. Coming straight to the point, since otherwise I felt I mightn't manage, I said our marriage was going through a very bad patch, we both knew that, and I was frustrated. Well, we had always said we would be honest with each other, and so now I was telling her I was going to be unfaithful to her.

'You what!'

The fact that she was so incredulous galvanised me. Hadn't she seen it coming? Determinedly I began to explain. I had never had another girl apart from her, had I? We had been going out since we were seventeen, for God's sake. And I had never had much fun in life with going straight from school to university to job, because so desperately in need of money. I felt I had missed out on something. Everybody had more than one lover these days. Most happy marriages were the result of both partners having already sown their wild oats as it were. Now I was going to be unfaithful. I had a girlfriend.

'Why are you telling me this?' she asked, almost gasped. It was as though she'd been living in a different world.

'I've always believed in discussing everything,' I said. 'It's you who always refuses to talk openly. I wanted you to see how dire things had got. I wanted you to understand.'

She shook her head fiercely from side to side, sat down, stood up, turned round, fidgeting her hands. She even laughed. And she began to tell me how weird I was, how I had simply sucked up my mother's mad piety, my Grandfather's coarseness, my sister's naïvety, my aunt's dumbness too. I should listen to myself. Boy, oh boy, should I listen. I was a bundle of contradictions. I was crazy. How could I announce I was going to go and have it off with somebody else and then try and defend myself. She got angry. When I wouldn't reply, she suddenly quietened down and said flatly:

'So it's the end.'

We were in the living room and I remember we both kept moving rather awkwardly about, not wanting to face each other. When she turned her back to look out of the window I saw her shoulders were trembling and this filled me with tenderness.

I said what did she expect me to do, the way she'd been treating me these past months? Really, what did she expect?

Shirley was silent.

'I don't love her,' I said. 'I just feel I have to have some fun. I'm living in a tomb here.'

She burst into tears. But this time my teeth were already gritted. I stood firm. She said if only I'd leave her and our bloody 'relationship' alone for five minutes, perhaps everything would buck up.

She stopped speaking and cried, still facing the big, rather clumsily double-glazed window where dusk was drawing the last colour from brown brick houses opposite. (Houses, houses and more houses. Everywhere people living together. How do they do it?) Then in a surprisingly sweet voice she said: 'Anyway, if you think I've changed since we met, what about you?'

'What about me? I haven't changed at all.'

'You were so fresh,' she said. 'You were so young. So urgent.'

70

'No one wants our marriage to work more than me,' I said.

'So don't go and sleep with this other woman. You said you didn't love her. I could understand if you'd fallen in love with someone, but otherwise, what's the point?' Then trying to change the tone of the conversation, she said: 'If it's fun you want, we can go and play crazy golf, for heaven's sake.' Because we had done this recently and really enjoyed ourselves, an empty Saturday afternoon in Friern Park.

'I've decided,' I said. 'Otherwise I wouldn't have told you. I wanted to be honest. I wanted to have this sorted out.'

Very quickly then, looking round her and picking up a few things, she went to the door and ran down the stairs. Her heels could be heard scratching like struck matches on the cement. From the window I watched her opening the garage door, her skirt lifting up the back of her slender calves as she stood on tip-toe a moment. She disappeared inside, then after a couple of false starts reversed out in her usual jerky way, clipping the kerb as she backed round. At the end of the close, indicating left, she turned right and was gone.

A Massive Change of
Position and Principle

For the first time in some years, as the car accelerated away, I cried myself. Perhaps she was right. It was the end. Though I very much hoped not. Later I prepared myself a couple of scrambled eggs, reflecting that I'd have to set the alarm earlier than usual in case I had to go to work by bus. Shirley had presumably gone to her mother's new and unnecessarily sumptuous flat in Ealing (the money that would have bought us our own place) and might well spend the night there, leaving me carless. I phoned a few times, but only got the engaged signal. Now I was getting used to it a little, I didn't feel so unhappy with the new situation. At least there were signs of life, an explosion of drama after what had seemed a life sentence of static friction.

And the following evening, after bowling (yes, bowling!), then dinner, then Rosemary's place, the advantages of my strategy became all too apparent. I had nothing to gain from not pursuing my goal to the limit now. So there was no hesitation. At my bright and chattering best – I felt seventeen again, but with the advantage of years of experience – around midnight I got Ros (as she asked me to call her) onto a rather Bohemian mattress on the floor (surrounded by mugs, wine-glasses and discarded clothes) and despite my delirious excitement at this new and so different body performed not at all badly I thought.

I returned on Sunday evening to find a note which read as follows:

George, please, this is a nightmare. George, we can't let our marriage end this way. We can't. I know it is partly my own fault, but I can't help it if I've been feeling depressed. I didn't tell you, but I have been to the doctor about it and to a psychoanalyst, you got me so worried that I might be mentally ill in some way, but both of them told me there was nothing wrong with me. There's a point at which unhappiness is just unhappiness in the end, frustration just frustration. George, I know that when we were younger, at university, with Jill and Greg, when career and work and all the foreign trips we were going to make seemed so important, I said I didn't want children. I said I was worried about nuclear war and so on and concerned about what sort of society our generation's kids would grow up in. Silly things to say really. Now I just know that I want children, my own children. I know that that is the way for fulfilment for me; honestly, I'm just not interested in a career of any kind. I appreciate that you can't possibly understand this *physically*, I mean the way I feel it in myself. How could you, being a man? But can't you accept it as a lover and husband and friend? Okay, I take your point that I promised. But it was an ignorant promise, it was like promising not to eat before you know what hunger means. Can't you see? You've become so hard, George. Why not soften up, please? Come on, be my bright handsome, hard-done-by, will-make-good little Methodist again, then let's forget the whole thing and head off on that holiday together.

All my love. Still!!!!

SHIRLEY.

It was nine o'clock. I phoned at once. She arrived forty minutes later. From the tone of that letter and then her broken voice on the phone, I had imagined her bedraggled: jeans, a sweater, tennis shoes, tear-streaked cheeks, little-girlish. I had imagined we would cry together and both plead *mea culpa*, then laugh and think how crazy we'd been. That was what I expected, and at least partly very much wanted. Instead she was carefully made-up, her lips were glistening and she was wearing a new twenties-style cylinder dress that frocked out just above slim knees, her feet pointing carefully in sharp white high heels, likewise new. There was something glassy and brittle and untouchable about it all, but stylish too; it suited her shape, her thin face and round wide eyes. She embraced me.

'Shirley!' I sighed. I get these waves of emotion sometimes. I just want to be very sentimental and have everything settled and happy.

But the embrace was brief. She sat down and crossed her legs, leaned forward, enunciating very correctly, as if at an interview or addressing a mixed race audience. She said: 'I'll stay, or rather you'll stay as long as you give up the idea of other women. Otherwise you'll have to go.'

Looking back, and considering my mood on seeing her walk into the flat at once so vulnerable and stylish, I'm sure this is a concession she could easily have wrung out of me, had she only had the sense to approach the matter differently, that is seductively, kindly, with comprehension. But the idea of going straight back into conflict and being simply bulldozed into concession was simply not on. It was thus with a wisdom that surprised me, worthy of my mother I thought, that I said: 'Shirley, honestly, there are so many things wrong with our relationship, the only hope we've got is to live together happily for a while. Then maybe we can make concessions. I mean, it's a long process. You have to work for it.'

'Oh, so for now we just kiss and make up,' she said. 'Is that it?'

'But isn't that what you said in your letter?'

'As long as you promise,' she said. 'But I'm not going to be treated like a doormat.'

I stood up. Somehow I felt as if I was acting, very aware of my position in the room, of what I was doing with my body, my hands. It all seemed very unreal. Not an unpleasant feeling, but a shade disturbing. I gave the wall a soft punch. I said look, look, if what she was really trying to tell me was that she wanted children and a happy traditional family, then simply to play it extremely slowly, extremely sweetly, and I might give in, probably would in fact, yes, most men did in the end, didn't they, but for the moment I was afraid that a baby would simply bind us together all the more, precisely when there were very clear signs that perhaps we weren't really suited to each other. Wait just a few months, I said. Hang on.

Would Shirley notice if the sun rose in the west? One wonders. Certainly on this occasion she didn't appear to appreciate what a massive change of position and principle I had just offered, what a major climb down this was.

She lit a cigarette. 'Unless you promise not to go to this other woman again, then you're going to have to get out of this flat and go and live on your own.'

'Shirley,' I said, 'we're both tired, we're overwrought. Now let's just go to bed and sleep on it. I've got to go to work in the morning. You're on holiday. I'm not.' (School had just broken up.)

She said the last thing she wanted to do right at the moment was be in the same bed with me.

'Suit yourself.'

But in the middle of the night she must have slipped in under the covers because I woke up with a start to find her clinging to me. She was naked, which was unusual for her (she usually wears a rather unexciting blue cotton nightdress). Not crying, not saying anything, she twined herself round me. So that when I had fully woken up we made love, violently, with her on top, which again was unusual. And while this was going on I remember thinking with some euphoria, 'We're really living now, really living, a modern life, with passion, with intrigue!'

17 Ollerton Road

Exactly five days before our scheduled departure for Turkey, Shirley received a letter 'advising' her that due to cuts in government grants, etc. etc., her school was being obliged to reduce its staff by two and they thus regretted to inform her that she would be without a job as from the end of the summer break. For myself I couldn't help feeling that this was rather a blessing in disguise. My first big stroke of luck. Now she would be forced to go for something more stimulating where there were real career opportunities to be had, especially since she wasn't in a position to apply to most state schools, never having got her teacher training certificate. She could move into something like the media or marketing or business administration or product management. Which should force her to brighten up and most probably get over the baby business.

But Shirley took it all very badly. On first showing me the letter when I arrived home from work, she was frantic and it was clear that she had been crying for much of the day. I honestly didn't know what to make of it. Trying without success to comfort her, I said laughingly that for the tough intellectual cookie she had always been, she was crying rather a lot lately, wasn't she? She went and locked herself in the bathroom. Not for the first time I experienced that acute, that lacerating awareness of having in all probability married the wrong woman.

The curious thing being that whenever I have this sensation I immediately do my utmost to repress it, I simply won't accept it, even now, and I get into a veritable frenzy of activity in an attempt to put things right and 'save the situation'. So now I looked around and started preparing a *spaghetti alla carbonara*, one of the few decent things I know how to cook, found a bottle of wine at the back of the larder, white, and stuck it in the ice-box, put a tablecloth on the table (took me a while to find where she kept them), sawed through a couple of frozen rolls and stuck them under the grill, etc. I made a feast.

When she finally emerged, I like to think lured by the smell of sizzling bacon, Shirley was thankful but still apparently inconsolable. It was the only thing that had been going well in her life, she said, her relationship with the children at school. The only thing that hadn't turned sour. And just to lose it like this . . . Everything, everything was going to pieces.

I tried to be cheerful, bustling with kitchen implements I wasn't quite used to. 'Think of it as a challenge,' I said. 'Get yourself a good job.' But she said that was another thing, she couldn't get herself a good job now, could she, because if she did she'd never have a child. You couldn't take a job and then go and get pregnant in the first few months, it wasn't serious. And she just didn't want to leave it for a couple of years more.

I sympathised, though privately I'm thinking, Come on, buck up girl! I mean, if something like this happened to me, I know I'd bounce right back, go for it, don't let them get you down. Where was her *joie de vivre*, for heaven's sake? She was only twenty-eight. And the following day, overtaken by a sudden summer horniness urgent as thirst, and seeing as I hadn't actually promised anything to anyone just as yet, I left the office early (thinking, after all, we'd be on holiday next week) and went over to Willesden to see Rosemary.

Who had her period. Mistresses, one feels, shouldn't have periods. We kissed and sat and talked. She was saying (again!) how amusing my grandfather had been with all his navy stories and little jokes and she kept asking, rather pointedly I thought, about my family and job. When I tried to get away after an hour or so, she protested, she wanted me to stay the night all the same, period or no period, so that I finally had to explain what experience now tells me I should either have got out in the open at the very beginning or just forever and forever denied: that I was married (but that my wife and I didn't get on and were thinking of divorcing, etc. etc.). Rosemary told me to put on my jacket, pick up my flowers and my bag and get the hell out at once. Just get out. Which, after only a second or so's lightning quick thinking, I decided to do.

I drove home and gave the flowers, fortunately still in their wrapping paper, to Shirley, which did have some cheering effect. But it was a day of incredible blunders. For, embracing me to thank me for the flowers, she sniffed the perfume an earlier embrace with Rosemary had left. (Women are so sharp with perfumes, whereas to be honest I can barely tell one from the other, they all smell of sex to me.)

I confessed at once. As I said, I was determined to be honest if nothing else. This time she didn't cry but was extremely cool and collected.

'So out you go.'

She went into the bedroom and started piling my stuff into suitcases. I refused to take any notice and sat down in front of some programme on geriatric care, which again had me wondering whether it wasn't time to dislodge Grandfather and sell Gorst Road.

'Out,' Shirley reappeared. 'Your bags are in the hall.'

'Where to?' I said.

'Wherever you like.'

'Shirley,' I said. 'Come on, we've been through all this. Please be reasonable. Anyway, if I go, how are you going to pay the rent, now you haven't even got a job? Then we're supposed to be on the ferry Saturday morning at ten.'

'Out.'

She sat down, leggily cross-legged on the floor and started to stare at me, while I continued to watch the television. She stared and stared, having me feel the full pressure of a gaze I refused to return. Then she had just opened her mouth to speak when the doorbell rang and it was Mark and Sylvia with their usual bottles of beer. And for once they were warmly welcomed, by both of us, as if by prior agreement. 'Oh hello, old mate, great to see you! Great!'

For a couple of hours we sparkled, we talked about the old woman downstairs who had taken to moving her furniture about in the middle of the night, the guy in the next block who put a blanket over his Maxi even in summer, about the three hundred Sri Lankans moving in at number five; Shirley rustled up some very attractive cheese and salad snacks on hot rolls; it was all perfectly charming, and even after they left nothing particularly unpleasant was said. Just that the following evening I had barely clattered through the door, before Shirley was barring the passageway announcing she'd found a room for me, in Southgate.

'Out,' she said. She put two freshly cut Yale keys on the top of the sideboard. '17 Ollerton Road. You can find it in the *A-Z*. The first month's rent's paid. Now go.'

I didn't think. Without a word, grim-faced, grabbing destiny by the scruff of the neck, and mainly just to show her I didn't give a damn, I picked up the suitcases, picked up the keys, which had the address and various other bureaucratic jottings attached to them on a luggage tag, and bumped downstairs. At least I got the car this time.

The room was what you might expect, one of London's endless makeshifts, a grand old Victorian house, now eight separate bedsits. My predecessor, I saw from the bells on the door, had been called Ms Deborah Samberuts. Well. I climbed to the third floor and found a single divan, chest of drawers, wash-basin, wardrobe, etc., all perfectly clean and irretrievably shabby. The pull-down blinds were broken. The walls were grey. A Picasso poster had been mended with Sellotape some long brown time ago and there was the dense smell of aerosol air freshener engaged in unequal combat with years of tobacco smoke stale in a tufty carpet. I looked round, smoked a cigarette myself to sort out the pong, then left my suitcases and went out to find a pub and eat something.

I think perhaps for three or four hours then I really believed that this was it, that we had separated, that I was going to live in this squalid room for a month or two before finding something more suitable and generally starting a new happier, healthier, or at least less stressful life, preferably as near as possible to the office, Greenford perhaps or Perivale. Rent a flat, fill it with appliances, pick up a really good car on the never never, I quite liked the look of the new Audi 80.

I closed the door and set out. The evening air had a cool but summery smell walking down to the main road; I interpreted it as a smell of freedom. The pub was full of young people who, from the volume of their conversation, the haze of smoke and maze of glasses around them, obviously shared my belief that life was for friends and fun. At one point there was a flurry of back-slapping and shouts. I sat on my own and watched animated faces, the shifting and posture of bodies, attractive and otherwise, and I must say I took a sort of quiet, determined pleasure, watching these people drink and talk.

However, towards midnight, alone in Ms Samberuts's room, when it came to unpacking what Shirley had put in those suitcases, finding toothpaste and pyjamas, a half-full bottle of Milk of Magnesia, my athlete's foot powder, I don't know why but I was simply overwhelmed by a great flood of emotion. I bit the pillow and wept. Physically I felt thoroughly sick, with a strain about my throat, tight chest, aching muscles. I beat my fists against the mattress and roared.

One wonders now about these explosive, these absolutely debilitating emotions: a fully-grown man lying in a shabby suburban room moaning. One wonders if somehow they mightn't have been controlled, tranquillised, fended off. For looking back, here was an escape route I would have done well to have taken. For Shirley's sake too. For everybody's. The irony being that I often wonder if these tumultuous feelings of regret, of sentiment, gusting through me like storm winds the way they do, aren't perhaps after all the best part of George Crawley, the nearest he comes to love. And equally frequently I will catch myself wondering if Hilary isn't my destiny somehow, if my present dilemma, which arose out of that crisis, isn't precisely the decision I was born to make.

I don't know. The superstitious mentality dies hard of course. In any event, I wept on the bed in this rented room, tried to sleep, couldn't, then did, and promptly had one of the truly atrocious nightmares I would later have to learn to get used to.

Mutilation is my forte with nightmares. It begins as a suffocating sense of horror, concentrated about clenched jaw and tight Adam's apple. Then all at once I'll be aware that, for example, my hand is missing. There is just the wrist dripping blood, perhaps the bone protruding, ragged flesh. Following which we plunge into hectic, gorily visual oneiric narrative as I feverishly wrap the stump in a blanket, in toilet paper, and start searching for the lost hand, wondering if it can't perhaps be saved, re-attached, my mind actually flicking at tremendous speed through all the sensational stuff one reads in papers about surgeons working all night to put some child's arm back on – always a child's. And in my dream, strangely, I am both a child and an adult, as if I had lost this hand years ago, yet the wound is still bloody and fresh.

I search. Gorst Road. Always Gorst Road. Sometimes it's my hand I'm after, sometimes my foot or leg, sometimes my dick, or even my head. Like some horrible ghost, I hunt through room after room, turning over settee cushions, opening drawers, the way in waking life I frequently look for keys I've mislaid, pens, papers, tickets. But the missing part is never found, just as the accident that caused it is never explained. And perhaps as I search I don't really want to find it, thinking how gory it will be when I do, remembering a book I read once where somebody digs his murdered child's head from a shallow grave, the eyes full of mud. Or on other occasions the search will turn up not the missing part of me at all, but Grandfather, gross and bloated in his armchair, or Aunt Mavis of all people, on her back, nightdress pulled up over a thick white belly, face hideously giggling in death.

Such is my average nightmare, the kind of neurosis-generated angst fantasy that merely confirms one's con-temporaryness, I suppose – busy man, under pressure – the kind of thing you can even learn to look on with a certain affection after the nth recurrence.

But the night Shirley threw me out was the first time. And the interpretation seemed obvious. I was mutilated by this break-up. Indeed in my sleep I started calling out for her, needing to show her the disaster, the bloody stump, and so finally, shouting my wife's name, I woke myself up. I was in a sweat, shocked and full of adrenalin. Immediately, in just pyjamas, relieved as I moved that I hadn't stopped to agonise over this one, I ran down two flights of gritty, lino-covered stairs to a payphone on the first landing. Then back to my room for a coin, then back to the phone.

I wept as I spoke. She wept on hearing me weeping. We told each other we couldn't bear the thought of separation. We had invested so much in our marriage, our identities were so wrapped up in it, in each other, we just couldn't bear for it to end. Who were we if not our marriage? In half an hour I was home and enjoying precisely the sentimental reconciliation I had hoped for and been denied just days before.

So that only a few weeks later, shortly after our return from Turkey, it would be the rings in her urine in the middle of the night, followed by the serious talk with Mr Harcourt, the mortgage, the payrise, the house in Hendon with permission for an extension, nausea, pregnancy books, pre-natal classes and a host of purchases to be made . . .

Such was the power of love. And now it actually came to it, I didn't mind. I thought, you can handle this, George. You can be happy with this. This is the way life goes. It's manageable. For Shirley was in such delightful mood now. She was so bright and pleasant, so much my old Shirley. And I thought, you should have caved in on this one ages back, George. This isn't going to do you any harm. When we lay in bed one night going through the Penguin book of names, I said: 'If it's a girl let's call her Hilary.'

'Why?'

'Because it means cheerful, apparently. Like us.'

Part Two

HILARY

How Things Happen . . .

There is a taboo about handicapped children of course. I've
had time and occasion to think about this. Either they are wept
over by social-consciousness mongers who want to show the
government's not spending enough, or they are simply not
mentioned at all. Except perhaps in jokes of the worst taste.
Their parents are generally perceived as angels who love them
against all the odds, or devils who abuse and abandon them.
Martyrdom and brutality make good copy. Another focus of
occasional interest are the ones who overcome horrendous
difficulties to paint Christmas cards with a brush gripped
between the second and third toes. Maybe the TV'll show
you about thirty seconds of their sad and twisted bodies (not
that I'm saying they should show more). Then there are the
tabloid fables of what genetic engineering may be able to do
in the future, and of course the emotive question of whether
the severely mentally handicapped girl should be sterilised
regardless of consent, that's an interesting old chestnut. But
the day to day business of working, nursing and cleaning, while
all the time facing that enormous sense of loss, of no hope, of
no way out . . . forget it. I certainly would if I could.

I was kissing Shirley's wet cheeks, she was squeezing my
hand hard, sobbing for joy. The child was born. Our child.
It was a girl. And so Hilary. We felt extraordinarily whole,
fulfilled as a couple, we really did. I was truly happy. When
the young doctor, examining the child on a white cloth, says
in the kind of regional accent one has come to associate with
sit-com and soap opera: 'It's a right mess this one I'm afraid.
Never seen anything like it.' Doctors, I've discovered, have
quite a way with the handicapped.

How things happen and one is tricked into getting used to them! My mother, bringing flowers and baby clothes, says she's sure it's nothing they can't put right. They can do such amazing things these days and we must all pray. Deliberately, I sense, she keeps calling the child by her name, as if she were already a person, picking her up, kissing her, celebrating, as if everything were perfectly normal. Immediately I'm aware of an undercurrent of pious persuasion, to accept this child on any terms as one of the flock, which immediately, instinctively I resist. Then resist the resistance. She is my child. So that I too say, 'Darling little Hilary,' while my mother kisses and fondles her.

But Shirley is listless. She keeps her baby completely swaddled and leaves it to the nurses to change her. She doesn't seem to want to touch or look at her. She doesn't want to talk about the problem, nor to hear all the rumours of syndromes, cures and prospects that I am rapidly gleaning. I sense that in her silence she is simply willing for it not to be true. She is waiting to wake up into a different reality. Breastfeeding, she weeps quietly, smoothing the child's thin damp hair. The little face is strange, and strangely endearing.

Mrs Harcourt arrives at last. She bustles brightly but keeps her camera in her case. She doesn't ask to see the girl's body. Mr Harcourt comes, phoning first to make sure he won't find Mrs Harcourt. He is grave and distant. There have been, he says, no cases, to his knowledge, of handicap in the Harcourt family. In the corridor he tells me confidentially that any way he can help financially not to hesitate to ask, and he claps me on a shoulder and says if anybody is equipped to deal with a problem like this it is me. I am so straightforward and sensible. I have my head so firmly on my shoulders.

Shirley's brother Charles surprises us with a first visit in ages and says he'll check up what benefits the government has left intact and we'd better grab them before they disappear. Shirley flares up and tells him to get lost. I feel this is a positive development, though when she goes to the bathroom I tell him by all means to do all the checking up he likes. We'd be grateful. 'The whole game,' he says, 'with the Welfare

State, or what's left of it, is knowing what's due to you.' I remember the waiting room of the clinic where we attended our pre-natal course and above plastic pigeon holes, the sign: KNOW YOUR BENEFITS. These brief imperatives. Somehow it reminds me of my mother saying: 'Couunt your blessings.'

They are doing tests, so Shirley has to stay in hospital. They have moved her and the child to Great Ormond Street. They take X-rays and do scans. They are trying to decide, they say, whether maybe an operation wouldn't put it right. But they have never seen a child with its feet the wrong way round before. Also the thighs are disjointed.

I tell Shirley I suspect we are being drip-fed the bad news at the speed they imagine we can handle it. Whereas I want to know everything now. She shrugs her shoulders. She says she has enough to cope with without my paranoia.

I take a few days off work to think. Already I am aware that I must decide on some strategy, some plan, not just let events take over, especially with Shirley withdrawing into herself. But to make plans I need information. I get on the phone and bother the specialists, the doctors, the ward sister. For God's sake, it's been ten days and still no sign of a diagnosis! Coming back from visiting, I stop at Dillons and spend half an hour picking up two hundred quid's worth of medical books. When I come out into heavy rain they have put the old yellow boot on the car. One thing you soon discover about personal catastrophes is that they don't excuse you from any of the other rules.

Shirley whispers: 'At least we're close to each other, Georgie. At least we're close.' I storm out of the room to demand some information from somebody.

The doctors stall me. They say our child is perfectly healthy, eating well and moving her bowels, and there is no hurry. Later I wonder if this isn't all part of a strategy. By not telling me anything they offer me the role of relief, of he who has to busy himself bothering other people and their secretaries. They slot your shock into their little routines. They have a way of getting you through. Which you hate and cling to.

Peggy comes. She is leaving the hospital as I arrive and we have a coffee together in the cafeteria. She keeps waggling her big knees under the table so that our coffee slops. I ask if she is cold, and I ask: 'So what does Buddhism have to say about the handicapped? Are they reincarnated dinosaurs?'

She says: 'You know there's nothing I can say, George.'

'Mother's praying,' I say, 'so that's one angle covered.'

She says: 'So am I as a matter of fact. Aren't you?'

I say I thought the Oriental brigade didn't go in for that direct request kind of prayer. I thought it was all meditation and inward illumination.

She says: 'I may not do it very often but I've always prayed just how I like, thank you very much.'

She is wearing a loose lilac jump suit, an old fashioned blue spotted foulard tied under her plump square chin. She has let her hair grow a bit and it's chunky and messy. She looks slightly overweight, jolly, attractive, a very normal London mother. I think: her career has always been just being herself, rather than doing anything, achieving anything. She has no direction, no thrust. Warming her hands round her coffee cup, she tries to look into my eyes and smiles. I look at my Jaffa Cake. I say: 'I always knew you were the lucky one, Peg. Fancy being able to pray.'

'You couldn't lend me fifty quid?' she asks.

Driving home that afternoon I stop at a Tempo discount warehouse and picked up the best videorecorder they have, plus half a dozen films to watch. I dream that I have lost my leg. It has been torn from my thigh. And I look in the fridge, in the airing cupboard, under the bed.

What is Life Expectancy?

Finally there is the interview with the geneticist. He is portly, dark-suited. He hums and ha's and smiles. He has the manner of someone who has accepted that sensitivity is a necessary accessory to his profession but has never been able to master it. He describes the baby's condition as defined in the reports of the various paediatric specialists: the physical deformities, notably of the legs and the major joints, an unusual brain scan.

Which adds up to what, I ask. What is it? And what are they going to do about it? Shirley in blue dressing gown with tiny pink flowers is silent with the sleeping child in her arms. Snuffling in its sleep it might be any child.

'Slowly does it, chaps. One thing at a time.' He has the consultant's avuncular smile, calmly twiddling with a propelling pencil behind an unnecessarily large leather-topped desk. He draws a breath, knits his brow: 'Now what I want to put to you is this: can either of you recall any similar problem in your family histories? Anything at all. Think carefully now. Some aunt, uncle, great grandparents, anything.'

Perhaps it is his curious manner of addressing us as if we were five-year-olds that makes me fail to see the obvious. Behind him, across the courtyard, I watch a tiny oriental girl wiping condensation from a window with the sleeve of her green pyjamas. Shirley shakes her head. A cousin of her mother's had a child with problems, but that was due to a trauma at birth.

The consultant nods with pantomime gravity. I jingle change in my pocket.

'Well, have we got any brothers and sisters?' He raises

white eyebrows. 'And have they got children, yes? No problems with miscarriages, for example? That's often an indication that . . .'

'Mavis!'

Yes, Mavis. In one split second, one click of the interminable and generally uneventful ratchet of time, my whole life, childhood and youth, career and marriage, apparently so varied, changing, picaresque, so much my own to do what I want with, succeed or fail, all collapses, concertinas, flattens, into my aunt's flat and mooning face. And is no longer mine.

Aunt Mavis. Hilary. Past. Future.

Perhaps fifteen minutes later, leaving his office with its big desk, its framed photos of smiling but obviously wrong children (in bad taste surely), Shirley says: 'I think that's the first nice bloke we've spoken to. At least he told us something.'

But I'm moving in a trance. Like some insect who discovers colour and flight is just a dream. He is still a cocoon-trapped grub. How can I live with a repeat of Mavis? Plus physical deformities into the bargain. Worse than Mavis!

'Well?' When we get back to the ward Mrs Harcourt has arrived. Despite the powerful central heating she hasn't taken off an elegant cashmere coat.

Charles is with her and comes out with me, asking for a lift to Shepherd's Bush. A caucus meeting. What is a caucus meeting exactly? Taking him gives me an excuse for going straight on to Park Royal to tell Mother. Tell Mother it is her fault.

Tall, lean, glassy-eyed, unshaven, old leather jacket, narrow blue jeans, Charles begins talking about the ins and outs of some Labour Council committee he is involved in. I'm not paying attention and anyway he must surely have appreciated by now what I think of his politics. Eventually I cut in to say, 'But what on earth do I care about rights for black unmarried mothers? Don't they have the same rights everybody else does?'

His tic is to rub thumb and forefinger along either side of

his off-white teeth, an intellectual, concentrated look on his face. He says he's been trying to distract me. And begins to roll a cigarette. It must be a difficult moment for me.

I tell him not to bother. I don't want to be distracted. On the contrary. My particular style is to look at problems and deal with them.

Pushing in the lighter, trying to be clever, he says okay then I can try some lateral thinking, I can look at black unmarried mothers as a category similar to my own, another minority who need defending.

'I beg your pardon?'

I am a member of a minority now, he says, with a handicapped child. The only way to progress is through solidarity with other minorities.

I'm quite harsh. I tell him not to talk like an arsehole, it isn't as though the black unmarried mothers are spending their days worrying themselves sick about my plight, is it? Nor can they possibly help me. Or I them. Each to his own. Anyway, it's their own fault if they have kids, with the State positively hurling contraceptives at them. Whereas what's happened to us was pure bad luck.

He seems to relish my rudeness: 'How you get into the hole you're in is irrelevant. It's how you get out that needs attention. You have to pull together.'

He has a bony, slightly freckled, very intense face, Charles. When he speaks, it is always with the assumption that he has thought more, and more deeply, about the subject than you have. I suck my teeth and decide to let the matter drop.

But as we are nosing our way out onto Southampton Row, he remarks: 'Anyway, Shirley's going to see what it's like on the other side now, I'm afraid.'

When asked what he means, he explains, as he did in a pub almost two years ago, that Shirley has always had an easy life, never really got away from home to see what things are like for the underprivileged. She was always the favourite child.

I've got chewing gum or something stuck to my shoe which is bothering me with the accelerator. And of course I'm thinking how I'm going to explode with Mother.

'She's never really wanted to look beyond her middle-class horizons at the way people are suffering out there. It was the same when we were kids. She was always so complacent. Whereas the real truth about the world is suffering.'

'She gives a lot of money to charity,' I throw in from a spirit of contradiction, trying to rub whatever it is off on the rubber floormat now we are at a light.

'Not too tough a proposition, when you take eighty thousand off Dad to buy a house.'

'She could perfectly well not give it.'

'On the contrary, charity of that kind is a luxury. Makes you feel better. In any case, private charities only confuse the issue. The responsibility is the government's.'

As so often, it's not enough in life to have things happen to you. You have to hear people's opinions as well. I breathe deeply. I say: 'I'm perfectly willing to accept responsibility for my own problems. I don't see how the government can be held responsible for my having a handicapped child.'

'You won't be saying that,' he remarks, 'when you see how much it costs.'

I turn round to him in almost disbelief. He is calmly inspecting his nails, my *A-Z* on his lap, frizzled cigarette between thumb and index finger. He doesn't seem to appreciate how incredibly unpleasant he is being. Nor, for that matter has he made any comment on the pleasure of riding in a new Audi 80. So I put it to him point blank: given that he's hardly bothered to contact us over the last two or three years, why the hell is he coming and visiting almost every day now?

He says unperturbed: 'Because you need help. I want to help. I mean that's what I'm doing with the Council and so on. What's life expectancy by the way?'

'You what?'

'Life expectancy. How long's the girl supposed to live?'

This question wasn't actually mooted with the geneticist (why not?), but instinctively, from Mavis's example, I know to say: 'Normal.'

After a brief pause for an underpass, he says: 'Too bad.' And he says: 'No chance of a little overdose or something. You could speak to the doctors. Sometimes they do that for you in the hospital.'

Despite the wave of anger that rises boiling inside – this is my child after all – I nevertheless have to struggle to suppress the first dim inkling that Charles is right.

'Better for absolutely everybody,' he is saying. My grip tightens on the steering wheel.

A Precedent

By the time I drop off Charles and pull up in Gorst Road I'm thoroughly keyed up. But Mother is out at her Asian women's conversation group. For some reason this annoys me intensely. She should be around at a moment like this. Not out showing solidarity to another minority group.

So I set about Grandfather. I set about him at once. I don't think at all. He's sitting in front of the television, as he might have been twenty years ago, sucking liquorice, poking about in his pipe, his belt unbuckled, his waistcoat, his hairy porish face. Walking in, I'm swept by a feeling of staleness and frustration. This is the mollusc shell I never really left somehow.

With no preamble I put it right to him: 'Didn't you ever ask yourself what was wrong with Mavis?'

I cross over and snap off the television. 'Didn't you?'

'Mavis?'

'Didn't you ever wonder why she was so dumb?'

I shout. I suppose really I'm still reeling from the blow, it still hasn't come home to me. And in a way I'm enjoying this reeling, this disorientation, knowing that it amounts to little more than a grace period before I'll be obliged to get on with things and make decisions.

Perfectly lucid, he says: 'What on earth are you on about Mavis for? Do we have to pay something?'

'Mavis had a syndrome!' I scream.

It's infuriating, but the fact that you have to shout at him anyway because of his deafness, neutralises any effect volume would have on a normal person. It's like beating fists on a wall.

'You what?' He squints.

'I said a syndrome. A genetic fucking illness. And you should have found out.'

The room is staler than ever. The old man has cakecrumbs all over his lap. I think: this should have been over years ago, years and years ago, the stale farce of this pissy old man in this never-to-be-refurnished room. My mother has kept it going beyond all reason, because of her selflessness, her refusal to start a new, fresh, cheerful life. Dimly I sense that this is what is to blame for Hilary. This decaying, stinking existence is touching mine, tainting mine, dragging me down. Or that's how it feels. As if Mother were keeping those bad genes alive on purpose, because for Mother life, however awful, is everything.

He says in a growl: 'Our Mavis was all right till she took up with that Mormon fellah. She brought home a decent wage. Anyway, how's Peggy? Never bothers to visit, the little . . .'

'I said, Mavis had a syndrome and now my kid's got the same thing only a million times worse. Do you understand or don't you?'

His wrinkled, limp-balloon face stares. His Adam's apple shifts. Then, grinning foolishly, pushing his tongue about in slack cheeks, he tells me: 'Stick the kettle on, will you? I could do with a cuppa.'

Almost raving now, and at the same time perfectly conscious of the mad futility of what I am about, I begin to tell him what a completely useless, useless old sod he is. He had a deficient child and never bothered to find out why, never worried that the same thing might happen to his children, his grandchildren. For thirty years he sat around doing absolutely bugger all but eat and drink and smoke and wear my Mother to a rag. And now the last straw is that, having never been warned, without the faintest inkling, I've gone and had a child like Mavis, but worse than Mavis, I'm going to be dragged back into the same ugliness I fought so hard to get myself out of, just because I share the same stinking gene pool he gave me and nobody ever bothered to inform me about. Well at least he might have the decency now to lie down and fucking-well die and let those who know how to live get on with it without the burden of a filthy old albatross like him round their necks.

My blood is pumping. I have never shouted so loud.

'You're nuts.' He heaves himself to slippered feet and tries to push past me. 'You're loony. Get yourself some pills.'

I push him back. He sits heavily.

'I'll kill you if you don't listen.'

Even if he can't really understand, at least he is fully aware now. At least he can see I hate him. His scabby old face begins to register a creeping alarm, veiny eyes squinting through gathering cataracts.

'Can't you see you've ruined my whole life? Ruined it.'

But words aren't enough. I just can't seem to make them mean anything of what I'm feeling. I stand and stare at him. And with that lucidity that lies like deep water beneath the foaming surface of my rage, it comes to me that this has always been the source of my frustration when I argue. Words just aren't adequate. It isn't about words. None of it.

So I hit him. Instinctively. I take a great swipe and let the flat of my hand slap solid into his cheek. One is so unused to violence. He ducks his head down, yelling. I slap again and again. I kick his shin hard. In a sudden desperate movement, he jerks himself up and comes at me, arms flailing like an angry child, uncoordinated and helpless, cartoon-like. He lashes. I grab him by the shoulders and, throwing my whole weight against him, heave him bodily back. He collapses into his chair again, panting. I raise my hand to slap and he weakly pulls up an arm to defend himself. I brush the arm away and slap hard. We stare at each other, his old unhealthy face quivering with fear and incomprehension. God knows what I'm looking like.

Enunciating fiercely, I tell him, 'Now if you don't agree to go into a home, old man, if you don't just leave my mother be, then I'm going to come here every week and beat hell out of you, okay. I'm going to beat you to a pulp. Now get upstairs and wash your face and stay out of my sight.'

Muttering under his breath, but definitely defeated now, he struggles to his feet and limps out into the passage and off upstairs.

Left alone, I find myself trembling and truly truly appalled. Resting against the mantelpiece, I pick up a dusty Hummel of a small boy and two yellow birds sitting together on a country fence, their mouths wide open in song. How my mother loves these quaint images of innocence and happiness. An ice-cream van tinkles in some suburban distance, exactly as twenty years ago. And I draw breath. I try to steady myself. I feel deeply justified in going for the old man, yet can't escape the terrible ugliness of what I've done. Have I ever hit anybody before? Never. What am I sinking to? Yet the paradoxical pattern of this experience – justification followed by ugliness – is all too familiar (didn't I feel much the same after cheating on my wife: justified, ugly).

When Mother comes back I burst into tears in her presence for the first time since childhood.

'We were so so happy,' I weep. 'We'd really got so close together. Why did it have to happen? Why?'

Mother hugs me and repeats over and over: 'Bless you, my dear heart, bless you, bless you, bless you, my dear heart.'

Later, driving home, I reflect that of course I only let rip with Grandfather so as not to have to do so with Mother. It was an easy way out. For in many ways it is more her fault than his. A generation on, it was she should have known what to do, her I should have been shouting at. Yet I know I never will.

I get home, transfer a Heinz curry and rice from freezer to microwave, and while that's cooking look up Christensen's syndrome in the medical book I bought. Of one thousand eight hundred expensive pages, my baby girl's condition merits only six lines:

Rare syndrome of varying intensity involving multiple disabilities and/or deformities. Cases differ widely and little is know of causes. Affects only females, but may (or may not) be passed on by males. Possible manifestations: spasticity of lower limbs, malformation of major articulations, cerebral palsy (rare). May occur together with, or be mistaken for, Down's syndrome.

The phone rings. My mother's voice speaks breathily: 'Something's happened to Dad.'

She found the old man upstairs on the floor by his bed unable to speak or move.

'Dead?'

'No, he opens his mouth, it's just he can't speak.'

'Stroke,' I say. 'You . . .'

'Oh, sorry, that must be the ambulance already, I . . .'

I say to phone me just as soon as she's got any concrete news or needs help. Then I put down the phone and eat. Going about all the routine domestic tasks that evening, washing dishes, wiping surfaces, I numbly wonder whether Grandfather will manage to tell the powers that be that I beat him, or whether they themselves will find signs of violence. I feel nervous, faintly horrified, but there's a growing sense of grim satisfaction too. Surely now he will be forced into a home at last. I have liberated my mother. It is not a crime. On the contrary I have done something good.

A precedent perhaps.

Four Thousand to One

What happens over the following months is that Shirley gives up entirely while I throw myself heart and soul into saving the situation, into finding, no matter how far I have to go, how much I have to spend, some cure that will reverse our little girl Hilary's condition. My reasoning is that they can't know for certain that her brain is in the same condition as Mavis's. The medical books, when they mention it at all, say the syndrome is entirely unpredictable in terms of severity and areas affected. No one can really know how she will develop. She might have a severe physical handicap and a brilliant mind, for example. So perhaps, I think, there is still a chance for our daughter and for us. And if there is such a chance, however remote, it is my duty to go for it.

Shirley comes home after a month in hospital. She refuses to speak about Hilary's condition. She avoids wheeling her out where she will be seen by neighbours. She looks after her carefully but clinically, never complaining how difficult it is to dress her with her stiff joints, never making even the most remotely relevant comments. She is efficient, tight-lipped, mechanical, beaten.

'Please don't tell me,' she says quickly, when I begin about something I have read, some information gleaned. 'Please, I don't want to know, okay?'

I say how important it is for us to communicate, pull together.

She says: 'When a tragedy occurs there's no point in pretending it hasn't.' And she says I was right all along, we should never have had children, they're too risky. Never never never. She could have found a job at another school, or in business, in the end she could have done it. We could have been happy. It is all her fault.

But I say no, she was right. And I tell her how much I want a healthy child now. It was just sheer bad luck.

'Bit worrying,' she remarks, 'when we both start telling each other the other was right.' She looks up at me from plucking a thread on her blouse and half smiles.

'Everything will turn out okay,' I say. 'I was talking to a specialist who . . .'

'Please, George.'

Weeks pass. We don't make love for the unspoken fear of somehow generating another Hilary. The geneticist has said a one in four chance. Add that to the, what, thousand to one chance of getting pregnant despite contraceptives and you're talking about four thousand to one, the kind of odds you might never win at, but could perfectly well lose at. Lying in our bed sometimes, watching the evening shadows that stretch and flit, I will be urgently aware of our extraordinary isolation, from each other, from the rest of the world.

Still, I resist the temptation simply to work late at the office and absent myself from family life. When I am at InterAct I work hard, I plunge into work as into a warm healing bath, I seem to reach intensities of concentration, speed of operation, I never dreamt possible before, but I always make sure I'm home in good time. I think, we will come through even this, I will save little Hilary. I will. And I am terribly tender with the little girl, changing and feeding her myself since Shirley lost her milk almost immediately. Sometimes I'll be up half the night, heating bottles in the microwave. I look into her small, slightly fish-like blue eyes and wait, hope for the first smile.

Many men, I've heard, simply refuse to look at a handicapped child.

Of the relatives, my mother and Shirley's brother Charles are assiduous to the point of irritation. Mrs Harcourt on the other hand pays ever rarer visits during which she will talk eagerly about proportional representation and the advantages of using faster film, before making for the door with the near

panic of someone leaving a sinking ship. Mr Harcourt occasionally phones offering advice about specialists suggested by
his professional friends. He will look after the consultancy
fees. Peggy brings Frederick over at weekends and offers
to babysit Hilary so that we can go out together. Shirley
invariably refuses. She doesn't want to go out. She wouldn't
know what to do.

So that one evening I say, does she mind then, seeing as
she has company, if I go out myself? On the Finchley Road
I phone Susan Wyndham, my contact at Brown Boveri, a
small girl, almost plain, but with a certain glint in her eye.
My wife is away, would she like to go out for a drink? And
in a Hungarian restaurant off the Edgware Road we talk very
seriously and theoretically about relationships and faithfulness
and fun and what life is for. Discrete loudspeakers are playing
mazurkas. With make-up and washed hair, she looks better
than I'm used to seeing her and has a knowingly wry smile
as we wander around for a while under thin rain looking for
a decent pub. When I kiss her below her Willesden flat, she
comes back so fiercely I'm taken aback. But afterwards she
cries and pushes her face into her pillow and says she has a
fiancé who had to go to Australia for a year with his company
and she's been faithful to him for nearly ten months. Why,
oh why did she let him down now?

When I get home it's almost one. Charles and Peggy are
arguing heatedly about feminism, which Charles is fiercely
defending and Peggy fiercely attacking. Shirley has gone to
bed with a couple of Mogadon. Hilary has obviously shat
and they are ignoring the smell. I change her and re-make
her bed. I sit on the loo and stare at the wall for perhaps
fifteen minutes, then grit my teeth and go downstairs to
propose Glenlivet all round.

Charles says: 'Of course, it's not too bad while she's still
a baby like any other. It's when she grows up that things'll
really get heavy.'

Please

Shirley has always been against an operation, or at least not for it. But the doctors tell us that if the child is ever to walk something must be done. And if nothing else there will be the aesthetic effect.

However, they need both our signatures.

My response, being first and foremost a doer is, okay, try it, go for it, cut. Shirley, who, for all her bubbliness and energy when she's up, has a fundamentally passive streak to her, is not convinced.

'What's the use?' she says.

'What do you mean, what's the use? We've got to try everything.'

'But the girl is like that. I don't see what's to gain by chopping and changing her. It won't work.'

I ask her how can we go on, how can we go on with our lives if we don't believe the child can be made normal?

'You always set such store by normality,' she says.

'I should hope so.'

'We've lived without it before one way or another.'

I say there's hardly any point in bringing that up. That was an aberration. We've got over it.

'And this is a tragedy.'

'Right, so we've got to get over this too.'

She finds her wan smile. 'George, you don't "get over" tragedies. Haven't you got it into your head yet that this has really happened?'

I remark that we would serve the little girl better if we argued about the matter logically without attacking each other. Anyway it is she, it seems to me, who is refusing to find out what's happened or to look into it in any way, while I've been all over the place consulting authorities and books and talking to specialists and so on.

'But it's not the kind of thing you need books and experts to help you understand. It's simple, you just sit and look at it.'

We stare at each other. Her face is drained, thin, but with a kind of luminous serenity to it. Which is new.

'They said if they did the operation she might be able to walk, they might be able to fix everything.'

'They said not to raise our hopes. You can't refuse to live with things just because they're not normal.'

'We were so together, Shirley,' I plead, 'before she was born. We were so happy. Weren't we? If only they can sort her out, everything will come right between us.'

'It's a chimera.'

'But how can you know?'

'Because they'd never have offered an operation if you hadn't bothered them so much.' And she says: 'I don't want her hurt any more than she is now. God knows what they'll do when they start cutting. She'll be strapped up for months. Nor do I see why we have to operate on her to improve our relationship. Which is fine as it is.'

My mother comes round and over tea and angel buns, brought in a biscuit tin I remember from earliest childhood, she begins to say what marvellous marvellous things surgeons can do these days. She's been praying so hard and it's true that the Lord is capable of revealing himself through science, His healing powers. She is sure it will come good.

Shirley asks how Grandfather is and says I really ought to go and visit him.

I phone Mr and Mrs Harcourt, Charles and Peggy, and get all of them to put pressure on Shirley. Everybody is on my side. Everybody supports the quick fix-it drama of orthopaedic surgery. Intervene, is the general chorus, do something about this wrong child, heal her, quick. And they are right. If the doctors are offering hope, who are we not to grasp at it? What kind of life could I have without it? Every time I come face to face with Shirley's entrenched fatalism, her 'accept, learn to live with it', I find myself feeling quite sick. I know I'll break down. I know that this is not my life.

The day before the operation Hilary smiles for the first time. She smiles and keeps on smiling. She beams from an apple-red complexion lying in a carrycot on the living room sideboard. The sight of this personality shining out of the so slightly strange face is at once immensely exciting, and distressing.

The same afternoon Mother phones to say that Grandfather is speaking again. They are moving him to a rehabilitation ward. 'He asked after you.'

'Oh really. What did he say?'

I notice that I'm not flinching at all.

'Just your name. He's not very coherent. Oh, and he asked for his pipe of course.'

'Are you pleased?'

'What do you mean? Yes of course I'm pleased. I was thinking perhaps it's a good omen for Hilary's op, love.'

Occasionally she does give away that it's all pure super-stition.

Hilary is ten hours in the operating theatre, far longer than they planned. Afterwards the doctors aren't even encourag-ing. The assistant surgeon, with a frankness I have come to prefer to the usual flustering for an improbable sensitivity, says he didn't find a single bloody tendon he honestly rec-ognised. Coming out of anaesthetic in the early hours, the child begins to have very severe fits, contortions, retching. Shirley phones me towards midnight, fearing she is going to die. I drive back to the hospital and we pass the dawn pacing a corridor and occasionally peeping in at a now heavily sedated baby.

In the morning I drive straight from Great Ormond Street to InterAct which has its offices in Hammersmith now. I press for extra sugar and look out through dirty panes at the huge black thrust of the Cunard Hotel, the lively, grey-gloss bustle of a summer morning in London. I realise I have been more than half hoping through the night for the easy drama of a death which would attract sympathy from all and generally make life possible again. Even now I imagine Shirley calling and telling me it is all over; I think how careful I will be to express no sign of relief. On my Filofax, to some unknown deity, I write the word: PLEASE.

How Do You Feel
About Your Life?

Grandfather has accused me of trying to kill him. The nurses are assuring Mother this kind of delusion is entirely normal, indeed is one more reason why he really ought to be in a home now. I say perhaps I shouldn't visit if it is going to disturb him.

So at least that side of the story seems to be working out happily enough. After just a few weeks on her own, Mother is already in better form than I can remember and since Shirley is out day and night at the hospital and seems likely to be so for some time to come, I accept her offer to come over to Hendon and cook for me. Thus when I get home of an evening she will more often than not be in the kitchen arguing with Charles about unilateral disarmament or euthanasia or privatisation, since Charles seems to be treating us almost as a home from home now (I really can't understand this). He will be sitting at table eating biscuits while she fusses with the oven or over the sink. Sometimes she brings a Filipino girl along to help, one of the walking wounded, a battered wife I think. She's a slip of a girl, dark, with a kind of furtive, injured beauty about her which I find rather attractive, though she never lets me get beyond the merest pleasantries before scuttling off to wherever her sad existence is based.

Despite the desperate situation at the hospital, this turns out to be really quite a pleasant time for me. A sort of hiatus. I'm waited on hand and foot. The house is calmer than when Shirley is around. There are even flowers Mother has picked from the garden, inexpertly arranged, but soothing all the same. Flowers are so alive and fresh in their stillness. Indeed, I can't remember when I last felt so free of tension.

And after Charles has finally pushed off with his politics and endless advice, and Shirley has called with the evening's last bulletin on Hilary's condition, Mother and I will have the most amicable mother-and-son conversations.

'Hasn't got over the fits yet?' she enquires. Her knitting needles click along the edge of a tiny sky-blue cardigan. Cardigans will be easier she thinks if the child has difficulty bending her arms. How easily she thinks these thoughts! Knitting she hums softly. Hymns. I recognise: 'Oh God our help', 'Lo, He comes', 'Immortal, invisible'. Quite.

I've got the TV controls in my hand and, flicking back and forth through channels from the sofa, surprise myself by reflecting that had I married my mother, or rather someone like her, all would have been well. Wouldn't it? I would have prevented her from spreading her generosity about too carelessly and she would have looked after me and generally agreed to do what I suggested, without the constant friction one has with Shirley.

Channel 4, I see, is illustrating the progress of the Spanish Armada with animated cartoons.

I say no. The girl has been at death's door all day. Severe spasticity. I dropped in on the way back from work and she was in an awful state. Shirley is barely sleeping. A consultant friend of her father's says that all the anaesthetic involved in such a long operation could cause brain damage in a child suffering from nervous disorders. Even cerebral palsy.

One says these things so calmly. And as I speak I do feel peculiarly calm. BBC2 is 'examining' safety in the air in the eager way journalists will. Should we be allowed to buy duty-free drinks? This is a burning issue. I fix myself a short.

Mother counts her stitches. She says: 'Perhaps it was wrong of us to agree to the operation. But I'd prayed about it so much.'

I have less trouble these days accepting the *non sequiturs* in my mother's conversation. One waits a moment as if to let a smell disperse.

On *EastEnders* some money has been stolen and race

prejudice is polluting the investigation. As well it might, frankly.

'It's so difficult to know what to do for the best,' she sighs. She begins to hum, 'Oh worship the Lord in the beauty of holiness,' reminding me of odd smells in choir stalls and paper pellets chewed from the corners of hymn books. Perhaps she finds the language on *EastEnders* hard to take.

'The doctors should have warned us. Charles was saying we should take them to court.'

'I can't quite see what that would solve.'

'We might get some money.'

It is her turn to let a *non sequitur* pass. Fair enough.

ITV are showing a couple of hippos in the incongruous process of copulating. A regular evening's viewing. I try:

'He also said it might be better if she died.'

'That kind of thing,' she frowns at her pattern, 'makes me very angry. You start with remarks like that and you finish up with Hitler and death camps. The little girl deserves to live as much as anybody else.'

It's curious. I am simultaneously thinking that Charles is right, but that Mother is also right. Yet surely they can't both be? Does the key lie in that word, 'deserves'? And why is everybody else so sure of themselves, so well defined? While I flounder. The press have been going through a phase of admiring people who have the courage to help their old sick relatives over the great divide. Selection of pills. The right mix. Contact the Euthanasia Society.

Upset by this kind of talk, Mother goes to the kitchen and five minutes later brings me some tea and fruitcake. Her light, flowery dress is hung with careful looseness about her bulk, her shoes are flat and sensible. One knee is visibly swollen.

Snapping off the TV, I find myself saying: 'How do you feel about your life, Mum?'

'How do you mean, love?' With a knitting needle she is scratching at the instep of a foot where veins bulge fiercely.

'You grew up looking after Grandad and Mavis. Dad gets killed after you've been married just a few years. Then you spend the rest of your life slaving for Peggy and me and

Mavis and Grandad and none of us were ever particularly grateful.'

'What a grim way to look at it,' she laughs. She seems not in the least perturbed by this, as she clearly was by the notion of mercy killing. 'No, I've had a very rich life. God has been good to me. He gave me a small ministry. I've been able to pray and have fellowship with all kinds of people and there has always been just enough of this world's goods. If you knew the number of times people have slipped things through the letterbox without leaving their names. It's been a very fulfilling life.'

Getting excited, I say: 'Yes, but Peggy and I didn't exactly turn out how you wanted, did we?'

'Oh, I don't know. Peggy has this nice boy Barry. You're happily married. I'm a grandmother twice over. What more could I want?'

Of course we both know very well what more. A great deal more. And yet I realise that this obstinately optimistic attitude is what I want to hear this evening. I want to hear my life described like this. And with tears suddenly in my eyes I find myself saying: 'You know, if it hadn't been for this awful business with Hilary, I would have loved to have had another child, more than one. What's one earning money for after all?'

Have I ever articulated this view before? Even with myself. It's perfectly obvious what one is earning money for: there's so much still to buy.

Her knitting needles click along the edge of a silence now welling with unexplained emotion; evenly and determinedly: clickety click, click and click, clickety click, click and click. Then she stops. She looks up from a face that age has rather bloated. She says very calmly: 'If you must know, dear, the one thing I regret in my life is the words they made me speak before they killed your father. I often wonder if they aren't somehow to blame.'

We stare at each other, in some amazement that this has come out. As if a ghost (my father's?) had crossed the room.

'You what? To blame for what?'

She sighs over the crumpled knitting in her lap, not tearful as sometimes in the past, but with a weary ravaged softness about her roughly-shaped features under their helmet of grey hair.

'For Hilary?' I put incredulity into my voice.

Unable to speak, she nods.

I jump up. For reasons I don't understand myself I'm quite ruthless. 'Don't be so bloody ridiculous, Mum!' One thing I am not going to do is be lured into her metaphysical scheme of things. 'You should see a psychiatrist. You know that? It's mad to think that kind of thing. Mad.' 'Dear George,' she's muttering. 'Dear George, I feel you're so near, yet so far.' 'No,' I say, 'the only thing you did wrong,' and I spit the words out, 'if you must know, was not getting Mavis thoroughly checked out. Okay? That's all there is to it.' And I'm stamping over to the drinks cabinet with at least a quadruple whisky in mind, when the phone rings.

'I'm bringing her home,' Shirley says.

I Will Hope

'I'm bringing her home.'

'What? She's better?'

Shirley is urgent: 'She's dying. I think they're trying to let her die here.'

I tell her not to be ridiculous.

'We'll need some oxygen. Apparently you can hire it. Check out the yellow pages.'

'But Shirley.'

'Do it. Now. I'll be back in an hour or so. I'll take a cab. I've already signed her out.'

'Let me come and get you in the car.'

'No. I've got to get out of here now. Please, George, get the oxygen.'

She hangs up.

Mother is blowing her nose, sorting out her eyes.

'Shirley's bringing her home,' I say, rising as one does to the drama of the occasion. In fact, while things are dramatic, life's generally plain sailing. I grab the yellow pages.

And so begins the great epic: the tiny baby running a high temperature, suppositories, constant changing of sheets, of clothes, of nappies, of dressings on her strange and butchered legs, constant forcing of bottles between clamped gums, followed by vomiting, contortions. Her skin is clammy with fever. She cries a shrill nagging cry. She fights, though ever more weakly, whenever she is touched in any part of her body, eyes almost always screwed tight, hotly red in the now wan wax yellow of her face. In her fits she will have respiratory crises which require the oxygen mask. An ear infection generates a constant flow of pus.

Grabbing a snack with Shirley in the early hours, perhaps the second night, or the third, while Mother watches over the girl, I say: 'We should have left her in hospital. They have all the equipment there.'

The house breathes silently about us. A hundred and sixty grand's worth now and going up around £50 a day. The kitchen curtains haven't been drawn and the yellow overhead light is hard and cold on the marble black tomb slabs of the windowpanes. Shirley's expensive pans are piled high in the sink. I stab at crumbs.

'Perhaps they were right.'

Shirley doesn't answer at once. She moves purposefully in jeans and tee-shirt, scrambling eggs. She is living in a constant state of nervous tension. She doesn't have the ten-hour escape to the office and other people that I have. Her face is drawn, gleaming with excitement. But she seems much more present, more decided, more one particular facet of her character than in the listless weeks following the birth. She is resolved, as if she had decided once and for all what to do, who to be. With a quick firm gesture she pushes unwashed hair from her face.

'Nobody,' she says, 'has the least reason for believing that Hilary will never think and speak and talk and laugh and sing. Why should we let her die?'

She is reasonable, sensible rather than aggressive, which makes it difficult to argue.

I say carefully: 'You didn't seem so concerned about her when she was born. I mean, a bit offhand and mechanical. Why the big change?'

She shrugs. She asks does she have to explain herself? She doesn't know. She might just as well ask why I have suddenly stopped hoping, since I was so hopeful and busy seeing specialists before. Arranging the operation. Wasn't I? And now I want her dead. That isn't fair, I say. We listen to the faint ticking of a wall clock. Then she says: 'I just want to see her smile again, you know. I rather fell in love with her when she smiled that day.'

Sitting down, she stares at me over the narrow table top.

Our faces suddenly seem very close to each other and large. I notice her nose is too red. She is ageing.

I say: 'Think of the pain she's in. Going on and on and on. Day after day. That ear problem she has. Her legs. Life is nothing but pain for her. It's unbearable even to think of.'

'The thing about pain,' she says, 'is that when it's over, it's over. But not being a woman you wouldn't know anything about that.'

'Let's not argue, Shirl.'

She smiles, stands up, leans over the table and kisses me. 'You've been wonderful, all the staying up you've done. I would never have expected it of you.'

'Oh thanks a lot.'

'Your mother too. Fantastic. Mine hasn't even come to visit.'

'Mum's in her element,' I tell her. 'She probably wishes it was twins,' and we both laugh.

Day after day then, nursing this sick child in a fetid, claustrophobic, overheated, over-emotive atmosphere. Two weeks, three. All taking our turns, shift after shift. Even the Filipino girl, Lilly, who will burst into tears occasionally and say how helpful it has been to find people worse off than herself, people she can help, how grateful she is. Peggy comes often. And Charles amazingly, an hour or two here and there, mucking in. People never cease to surprise you. If he does care for us in some way, then he certainly fooled me. I wonder will he use the oxygen if and when the child has a crisis in his sole presence. The question floats across my mind as an intriguing curiosity. The little girl's life hangs by the most snappable of threads. For myself, in the drama of our trance-like weary nights, I have decided I must be good as the rest, I must do everything possible to see the little girl through. I'm determined still to believe, or at least not one hundred per cent exclude, that she does have a chance. And while that is on the cards, I will, I will hope.

What a relief though when I go to work. Or to Susan's. Four, five times now. She always serves something of a feast after we've made love – eggs and bacon and beer and ice-cream. Traditional, solid fare. It's almost better than the sex. Coming home on the tube, I tear an article about euthanasia out of the *Standard* and slip it between the pages of a scrapbook I keep in my briefcase.

The Worst Betrayal of All

It's a few days after Hilary comes through her fever, that Shirley breaks down. The little girl's improvement is sudden and dramatic. The temperature falls, her breathing becomes even, and in the space of a few hours a bloom returns to her cheeks. We are euphoric. We open bottles of Oddbin's Verduzzo, we talk about the future, we jubilantly call the hospital to fix an appointment for the next check-up. Except that with this apparent return to health, we notice that the child isn't looking about her in the same way she did at two months, before the op. She seems unable to follow a finger, to see the teat of a bottle.

At the check-up, which a surprised consultant arranges almost at once, a paediatric optician is called and immediately confirms that Hilary is indeed not seeing. The eyes, he says, are perfectly okay in themselves, but not responding or focusing. Something in the brain. The consultant hopes, clearing his throat, fussing with a pen, that this will be a temporary 'symptom' due to post-operative trauma. 'You should feel very proud of yourselves,' he goes on quickly, 'I honestly didn't think the girl would survive.'

'Just that now she seems a great deal worse than before the operation. And her legs won't bend.'

This middle-aged man smiles. He is long-jawed, school-masterly. 'Actually, that remains to be seen.' He focuses deep-set eyes on me. 'I'm sorry, but this was not by any stretch of the imagination routine surgery, hence there were risks which we did warn you of. Certainly we don't take these decisions lightly. However, and be that as it may, we shall have to wait a good, what, at least six months more to know the real results of the operation one way or another.' He stops. 'Nor do I see any need to be too pessimistic. The child has survived after all, which shows remarkable resilience.'

Shirley says: 'She doesn't seem to be able to hold her head up straight, doctor. I mean, she should be able to do that at four months, shouldn't she?'

I haven't actually registered this myself before, but realise now that this is what makes the girl so odd. Even when you hold her up, her head will loll slackly to one side. And I have one of my sudden piercing revelations, visions, of what our life will be like from now on with this handicapped child. I see her at five years old, ten, her head lolling.

Shirley is nodding gravely as the consultant describes the special kind of chair we will have to buy in about six months' time to keep the spine and neck straight. Some kind of allowance, he is saying, is available to cover at least part of the cost.

Which is? Shirley is being very practical.

He doesn't know. About £400 perhaps.

We stand up to leave. Then no sooner have we got in the car than Shirley flips. She straps Hilary into her seat and bursts into tears. She howls: 'All those nights, all those nights of pain, and now she can't even see!'

I drive brilliantly fast. I'm getting to know the lights and lanes round behind the hospital. That splendid feeling of challenging the great city machine: filters, left-only lanes, bus lanes, bollards, no right turns, sequence-timed lights, brake and accelerate, brake and accelerate. I stay silent a long while.

'I can't stand it, I can't, I won't stand it.' She doesn't even fiddle with handkerchiefs, just weeps, shoulders shuddering.

Finally, caught on a long red, I say: 'Shirley, Shirley!'

'I wish I was dead,' she shrieks.

I drum my fingers on the wheel: 'We should have been angrier. We should have told him we'd sue.'

'God, do I wish I was dead!'

I storm up the Caledonian Road, jerking from pedal to

pedal. The motley buildings race toward us, the wheeling sky, the low neon, tall blocks of flats, the afternoon sun occasionally spangling on blank glass, the rubbish outside cheap restaurants, the usual motley on the pavements.

Our child is blind.

Shirley is moaning now. I can think of no other word for it, a low animal cry, her face in her hands.

Overtaking on the inside lane, squeezing back into the flow before a parked car, it occurs to me that driving is not unlike a computer game. Some program that would project your score onto a corner of the windscreen perhaps?

I say maybe it really is only post-operative trauma. How can we know? In any event we must find some other consultant to contact who will tell us more. 'These guys never tell us anything.' Maybe we can find out if there's some big specialist in America or Switzerland or something. 'You can bet they'll be light years ahead of the NHS for this kind of thing.'

'I wish we'd never met,' she says.

'Come on, Shirley.'

'Sometimes I hate you for all this.'

I don't object. I often feel the same.

We drive on with an urgency that scatters other traffic like confetti. She doesn't comment on it as she usually does. One secretly hopes for an apocalyptic accident of course. She leans over her seat and caresses the child's thin hair. She is murmuring now. I stare at the road.

Has my mother been working on Shirley these weeks she's been staying with us? I haven't actually noticed anything, but I often think Mother manages to exude influence even without speaking. Her eyes, her posture, her tone. She will persuade you to see the world as she sees it. In any event, when we get back home, Shirley carries the baby with her into the house while I stick the car in the garage, taking my time over everything now, relaxing, calming down, turning keys and handles with the slow, almost voluptuous pleasure I have recently begun to find in doing all those little activities that keep you just outside the family sphere: taking a pee, a bath, a shave, carrying the rubbish out to the bin, changing a lightbulb in an empty bedroom. I move with meticulous painstaking slowness, the exact opposite of my driving, though the escapist intent is no doubt the same. When finally I walk into the living room, Shirley is in my mother's arms weeping.

She is making some kind of confession. It is all her fault she is saying in a low voice broken by sobs. All her fault. She's been a terrible wife, she forced me to go and have other women, had an affair herself for ages and ages.

'Shirley!'

Instinctively I try to wade in and stop this, but she clings tightly to my mother whose large face watches me over her shoulders.

'It must be a punishment. It must. It's too awful.'

'Shirley, shut up!'

I start to shout, to try to pull them apart. Hilary wakes, as she always does, screaming. Through the bedlam, my mother says quietly: 'George, why don't you just go out for a while and let her get this off her chest.'

I hate, no really hate the attempt, inherent in that everyday expression ('get this off her chest') and again in her tone of voice, her willed serenity and motherliness, to reduce the whole thing to a kind of understandable outburst which will soon be over.

'No. It's ridiculous. Shirley. Don't be crazy! Let's talk this over on our own.'

My mother, her face half in Shirley's mussed hair, mouthes the word: 'Please.' Her old eyes, tremulous in their papery net of wrinkles, glow and plead, insisting I am her son. And I go. As much simply to be out of it as anything else. I go to Child's Hill Park and smoke about a hundred cigarettes.

When I get back, they are in the baby's room, kneeling and praying by Hilary's cot. They don't see me at first and I spy on them a moment from the landing. They are knelt in a clutter of toys and baby clothes on the carpet. The curtains must be drawn, because the light is pinkish grey filtered through red. My mother, on her swollen knee, has both raw hands hooked over the top rail of the cot, her face pressed against her knuckles, shoulders hunched, back bowed. Shirley on the other hand is kneeling straight up in perfect finishing school posture, girlish, virginal, the smart dove-grey wool dress she put on for the consultant falling prettily over her curved back, her slim calves; the fine ankles still in their white summer sandals. Then Mother launches into another prayer: 'Oh dear Lord who so often in the past . . .'

In bed I ask: 'You really had an affair?'

'Yes.'

'Who with?'

'A teacher at school.'

'When you were so depressed?'

She laughs softly: 'No, before that. I was depressed when I lost him.' She adds: 'I'm sorry, George.'

I take this in. After a moment I tell her: 'I don't blame you for that. But this with my mother is the worst betrayal of all.'

And next morning when I get Mother alone for a second I ask her please to go. I don't care how much help she is being, she'll have to go.

It is a Saturday and I spend the whole day cracking a computer game called Helicopter Attack. The sneaky thing is the way they keep altering the wind speed so that you drift off course into the flak. In the evening Peggy comes over with Charles and mentions almost in passing that Buddhist Barry, her lover of two years standing, has left her. The marvellous thing, it occurs to me, about Peggy is how she never needs comforting.

Flow Chart

Drama over, routine sets in; looking after this strange child who catches every possible infection, who is allergic to antibiotics, to food additives, who knows no difference between night and day; the progress of other children (Peggy's Frederick, Greg and Jill's Rachel, running, jumping, chattering, doing jigsaw puzzles) simply underlining this other baby's utter lack of it, can't roll over, can't hold anything, can't sit up; Shirley giving all her time, all her energy, the exhausting nights. At age one, eight months after the op, the little girl smiles again, she even chuckles.

'You see, she's happy.'

'Shirley, she's blind, she's immobile, she's utterly deprived.'

'But she doesn't know she is. In her spirit she's happy.'

I say: 'I smile a lot. At the office I even guffaw. I tell jokes. It doesn't mean I'm happy.'

'That's your problem,' she says. 'Or do you want me to kill you out of sympathy?'

She begins to find the most minimal signs of progress, an ability to clasp a hand around your finger, to move her head, just ever so slightly, when she's called. Sometimes. She doesn't attach disproportionate hopes to these developments. On the contrary, it's really a sign that she has accepted things. She is content with this much. The girl can clasp your finger. So there is something there. Some personality.

At nearly two the child learns to roll over. We can't leave her on the couch any more.

Stimulation! Yet another consultant expensively tells us what we've already read in books. And now I am encouraged to design 'computer games' for the child. Well, I'm willing to try. I start with a big board that straps onto the eating tray on her £500 chair. When she presses coloured knobs an amplifier plays different tunes and bright colours shine on our TV screen placed right in front of her. Perhaps she can see, just a little. Perhaps. I wire up a system of pedals for her feet, I make the controls of the hand-operated board more complicated so she has to manipulate them, to the right, to the left. This strange child giggles, hearing our voices around her. She gets excited, heaving herself about. And it is gratifying. Shirley is impressed, grateful. I become enthusiastic. Hilary is pressing the pedals. She is, somehow, with wrist and elbow as much as fingers, moving the knobs. On purpose or at random? Her face is blank apart from those sudden brilliant smiles. Which don't always seem to coincide with any visible stimulus, but does that matter? When I introduce a knob she has to turn rather than push she can't do it. Immediately she loses interest. If it really was interest. She bellows. Flails limbs. What does she want? Give her food? Her bottle? No, she spits it out and screams. Hug her? She bellows even louder. What then? I think, this child will be in nappies, at five, at fifteen. At thirty. While Shirley tells our friends: see the progress she is making, she can push these knobs, look, these pedals, she makes the tune play, the lights come on. I can see the pain in the visitor's eyes, the desire to change the subject, to head for the drinks cabinet. Even Peggy doesn't seem to want to hold the girl. She's heavy. With no real exercise she's getting fat. How loud will she bellow when she's twenty?

I am convinced I shall go mad. The sense I have of constant high tension in the jaws. The nightmares. And I now have a whole file full of euthanasia cuttings. I keep them locked in the bottom drawer of my desk. A woman in Carlisle has drugged to death a four-year-old boy terminally ill with bone cancer. The judge let her off with a suspended sentence. In Truro a man and wife are fighting because the wife wants their two-year-old comatose daughter taken off an iron lung and the husband doesn't. He's divorcing her over the matter and wants custody of the child. She's contesting it. She says she's the merciful one. In Dijon, France, a man butchers his new-born mongoloid with a pair of scissors.

I read these articles on the Northern Line. Never more than a couple of brief paragraphs, they nevertheless hold me spellbound the whole journey from Hammersmith to Hendon Central. In Rotherham a nine-year-old boy with severe muscular dystrophy claws his way out of his wheel-chair to throw himself from the third floor flat of the council estate where he lives with his unmarried, unemployed mother and alcoholic grandfather. Or was he pushed? And they're actually bothering to check! Yes, full scale police enquiry. Time, tax money. Is this the public good? Medical evidence shows signs of struggle. Mother says yes but she was trying to hold him back. I miss my station.

Hilary, I think, could never be imagined to have climbed to a window.

On the other hand she can't simply be switched off.

And I could never kill her with a pair of scissors. I love her.

This happens. I am walking back to the car in the tube-station carpark when I see a hoarding. It says: MUSCULAR DYSTROPHY: We Know The Cause, Now Help Us Find The Cure. What it shows though is three stylised green Plasticine figures. They are children. The two at each side are standing and reaching a hand down to help the third between them who seems to have stumbled and is crouching low. Tripped by the disease. Can they pull him up? Can they rescue their little companion? Buzzing open the car lock with the remote control, I burst into tears. I cover my face. This hopeless, stupid, heart-rending image of human solidarity. I feel so vulnerable. There is a Giro number to send cheques to, but I don't write it down. The illustration has already convinced me that there is nothing to be done but turn away.

Shirley takes Hilary to church. She has converted though there have been no more dramatic scenes since the confession to my mother. Quietly and conventionally (I almost said sensibly), she goes to church, gets involved in crèches, in organising the kind of charitable events I have avoided since I was fifteen. Occasionally 'church folk' drop round and make an inhuman effort, maybe twenty minutes, thirty, to give Hilary some attention. Occasionally I find Shirley in what can only be an attitude of prayer, usually by the cot Hilary is now too big for (but she would fall out of a normal bed). So, after all our laughter years ago at Mother's expense, Shirley has become a Christian. Whatever that really means. But she doesn't want to talk about it. Nor do I. Just once she says, 'However obscure, there must be some reason for this, some plan, there has to be. I do believe there has to be a God behind it all.' Just once I say: 'You can't honestly believe we're guilty and this is the punishment. It doesn't work like that.' She says slowly: 'I know. You're right. It's just that sometimes I feel that's how it was. I make that connection.' It seems pointless trying to argue the absurdity of this out logically, since sometimes I feel the pull of this explanation myself.

Typical scene. Shirley comes running, says excitedly: 'Hilary called me Mummy today.' 'Great!' But I know that if the miracle ever happened it will never be repeated. The girl may giggle when you soap her in the bath, she may randomly press those knobs I have provided her with and laugh at the electronic tunes that result, she may even be able to see just a little light and colour, but she certainly never calls her mummy, Mummy.

Dressed up she looks a plain ordinary little girl somebody has tripped up, floundering on her back. On a rare visit, Mrs Harcourt takes a photo of her against a background of Alexandra Palace flowerbeds.

And two hours physiotherapy every single day. It's a new American method. A trip to Philadelphia to gen up. We, or rather Shirley, bend her joints, roll her head around, knead her muscles. She screams throughout.

Will she ever be able to eat on her own? Even to bring a bottle to her lips? Who knows, but it has become Shirley's mission I sense. All the more conclusively and engrossingly, because it is a mission that can never be accomplished.

Is this the life she wanted? We wanted? Isn't it pathetic, creepy, giving so much help to a helpless case? Like my mother with Grandfather, with Mavis. Isn't it a way of giving up on that other, bigger life we should be living? Shirley is intelligent, attractive, *valuable*.

'Is this the life you wanted?' I ask.

'It's the life I've been given,' she says mysteriously.

'You sound like my mother now.'

'What's so bad about that? Your mum's okay.'

I don't say it, but I think, At least my mother's wounded can walk. For some reason I think of the Filipino girl.

The fact is that although Mother hardly ever comes since that day I told her to leave, Shirley spends anything up to an hour on the phone with her every other day. Talking about me no doubt, and about Hilary's 'progress'. Meanwhile, at the office, I draw up the following flow chart:

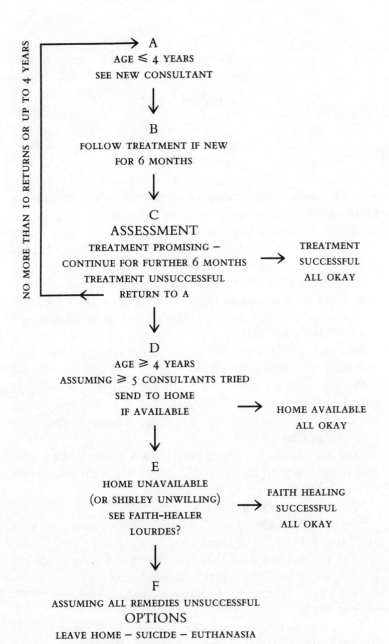

NO MORE THAN 10 RETURNS OR UP TO 4 YEARS

A
AGE ≤ 4 YEARS
SEE NEW CONSULTANT

B
FOLLOW TREATMENT IF NEW
FOR 6 MONTHS

C
ASSESSMENT
TREATMENT PROMISING –
CONTINUE FOR FURTHER 6 MONTHS → TREATMENT
TREATMENT UNSUCCESSFUL   SUCCESSFUL
RETURN TO A   ALL OKAY

D
AGE ≥ 4 YEARS
ASSUMING ≥ 5 CONSULTANTS TRIED
SEND TO HOME
IF AVAILABLE → HOME AVAILABLE
ALL OKAY

E
HOME UNAVAILABLE
(OR SHIRLEY UNWILLING) → FAITH HEALING
SEE FAITH–HEALER   SUCCESSFUL
LOURDES?   ALL OKAY

F
ASSUMING ALL REMEDIES UNSUCCESSFUL
OPTIONS
LEAVE HOME – SUICIDE – EUTHANASIA

What Heroes

I find it pretty funny frankly that it took an atheist like me to think of faith-healing. Still, weird things do happen. It would be foolish to pretend otherwise.

'But you don't believe in it,' Shirley protests, laughing.

I remind her that we have tried all the consultants, we have flown to Houston and to Geneva. We have blown upwards of fifteen grand. It's simply a case of trying to cover every angle. 'That's my way.'

She gives me her narrow look. 'What exactly,' she asks, 'is Hilary preventing you from doing in life that you would otherwise like to do? Why keep hunting for a solution you know isn't there? Come on. Tell me one thing she's preventing you from doing. Nothing. You see. You can't think of anything.'

I tell her: 'Look, Shirley, if Hilary wasn't here, I'd be happy to have another child. We could adopt one. I do believe we would be happy.'

'What do you mean, "wasn't here"?'

She knows perfectly well what I mean. Nevertheless, I say: 'If she went into a home.'

'But we've been over that a million times. She wouldn't get any attention. She'd make no progress.'

'She's not making any progress as it is.'

'Yes she is.'

My own inclination is to be honest about these things, however brutal it may seem. All the same, I say:

'If she were being looked after, you could get a job.'

'I don't want a job.'

'But you must want to get out of the house sometimes. Don't you?'

'Of course I do, but I can't and that's that, so what's the point of moaning about it.'

'You're denying yourself.'

'Yes.'

'For a creature who has no hope, no future.'

She pauses. She bites her lip. 'Not perhaps in the narrow way you define those concepts.'

'So how does Shirley Harcourt define them.'

'I don't. I just get on with things, that's life.'

'Oh, mysterious life again.'

'Right.'

Then she says: 'Anyway, what future do you have, George Crawley?'

'Oh come on.'

'You see.'

'I'm sorry, but I don't.'

'And didn't George kill the dragon to save the damsel, not vice versa.'

'What on earth is that supposed to mean?'

'I've seen your scrapbook,' she says, 'okay? And it's inhuman what you're thinking.'

I turn away. 'Only too human to go by what's written in those articles.'

I persuade her, after the ten consultants, at least to go and look at a home. Check it out. We drive up to the Penelope Hardwick State-assisted Charity School for the Severely Handicapped in Enfield. In the car she says chattily: 'I honestly can't understand what's eating you so much. I'm doing everything with her now. You have all the time in the world to do whatever you want. Leave earlier in the morning if you like, come home later. Work weekends. The world's your oyster, George. Go get it.'

I realise she is telling the truth. I mean about not understanding. She can't understand. This is the crux, she can't understand me. Otherwise she wouldn't say these things.

'And if you want some fun at least get yourself snipped

so we can make love. I could do with some action too, you know. Then we could go out occasionally if you want. Your Mum is willing to babysit. So's Charles, though I'm not sure I could trust him.'

'I don't want to see my mother any more than is necessary.'

She says not to be such a big baby. What does it matter if she knows we screwed around?

She doesn't understand.

'You're hung up,' she tells me then.

'Perhaps I am. But at least one should be able to count on one's wife to respect one's hang-ups.'

And when Enfield's one-way system at last allows us to find it, the home really is pretty awful. One storey, yellow brick, the windows blue metal-framed, black lino floors, walls green to waist height, white above, firedoors at regular intervals down an interminable corridor reeking of disinfectant; in short, the spaces, shape and general utilitarian meanness of any institution, rendered poignant in this case by worse than usual childish scribblings pinned on the walls, by a background smell beneath the disinfectant of shit, by the cluttering paraphernalia of the handicapped: wheelchairs, walking frames, lifting devices in the bathroom. And then, inhabiting this ersatz fluorescent-lit environment, the fifty hopeless, slavering, contorted, clamouring, spastic, clumsily-dressed, unkempt basket cases. I know, I know, but what else do you want me to call them? Do we have to be pious? Except that sometimes the eyes are so intelligent, the gaze so piercingly clear as they register your panic. One little Asian boy in particular. A tiny, horribly deformed monkey with huge gorgon eyes. Amused. He laughs when he sees me in my suit and tie.

But Hilary is not one of those. Her eyes don't see.

The white-coated staff are kind, bored, complacent, addressing the children with the same slightly sharp, patronising voice one might use for untrained pets or for the senile. Irritation, one senses, is kept at bay only by professional resignation. How else could it be? Much flustering to get a certain overweight Thomas to renounce a pen he is in danger of jabbing in his eye. 'Come on, Tommy, you've been such a good boy this morning.' Judging by his bulk, he's at least eleven, ugly and belligerent.

Shirley smiles readily. She doesn't seem to have the same difficulty simply looking that I have. Her manner reminds me of our pre-natal courses; she's fresh, gregarious. Immediately she plunges into earnest conversation with one of the younger 'teachers' on the kinds of handicaps, the types of treatment. How many hours of this and that do they do, staff/children ratio, frequency of parental visits. 'This child has Horner's syndrome.' As if we were connoisseurs. 'Yes, it's so exciting to see the progress they make, the way they come out.' What were they like before? A spastic boy, wrists unnaturally twisted, is incessantly fingering pouted lips, his face blank in front of a morning TV programme showing how tennis balls are made. The TV is high up on the wall, out of harm's way. In the corner a boy with only flippers protruding from his shoulders is trying to turn the pages of a comic book.

Of course these people must be looked after.

We are invited to stay to watch the children eat their lunch. I quickly invent a business appointment.

Silence in the car. I don't even bother persuading. Shirley is kind enough not to say told you so. What she does do though is whistle as we inch down Ponder's End High Street. She doesn't often whistle. I recognise: 'New every morning is the love'. She has recently joined the choir at St Barnabas. Apparently she sits at one end of the stalls with Hilary in her special chair on the chancel steps to the right. It is one of her illusions that Hilary appreciates music.

Finally she says: 'What heroes.'

I say: 'Yes, I was wondering why my mother never thought of it.'

Good Thick
Foil-Wrapped Chocolate

The first faith-healer I try operates from a semi-basement flat off the Fulham Road. She is not a big name. I go to this woman because the MD, Johnson, and his wife have been enthusing about her for months. Margaret, the wife, in her early fifties, is intelligent, upper-class, well-educated; a sceptical type I would have thought. For more than fifteen years she has suffered intermittently from severe back pains which sometimes make it impossible for her even to stand up. After innumerable medical examinations, tests, X-rays, scans, drugs, massage, acupuncture and even an exploratory operation, she was finally persuaded by a friend to try Miss Whittaker. In just three 'sessions' she was healed. She hasn't had the pain for months. So what did Miss Whittaker actually do? Nothing more than lay her hands on Margaret Johnson in a darkened room.

Normally of course I would take this kind of story with the very large pinch of salt it probably deserves. Menopausal women are famous for their psychosomatic problems. I've always given faith-healing about the same credibility rating as flying saucers and abominable snowmen. Things we'd like to believe in, good newspaper fodder. But at a price of £12.50 a session it is surely worth a whirl.

At the back of all my calculation there is always that faint, that constantly suppressed but in the end indomitable craving for a miracle, that residual part of me which is still a little boy kneeling in a cold church clutching at a thread of faith. Surely this is normal. The fact is I have made a sort of promise that I will become religious, Christian even, if a miracle occurs. 'Master, we would see a sign from thee,' I remember the verse from Sunday school. Who was it? The Pharisees? And what could be fairer? People have been doing these deals for centuries. If He wants my soul (if I have a soul), let Him show me a sign.

So I casually mention to Neil, the MD, who any day now will be inviting me to be a director (I have seen an exchange of memo's between himself and one of the non-executive partners), that my mother also has a back problem. (I have never told anyone at work that I have a handicapped child. Somehow I know it would be unwise.)

Having thus wangled address and phone number, I then have to persuade the fabled Miss Whittaker to give me an appointment on Saturday afternoon. Soft-spoken, the woman has the irritating habit of leaving long pauses on the telephone. She doesn't usually 'receive' on Saturday. She goes to see her mother in Richmond. I offer to pay double and to drive her on to Richmond afterwards if that would help. Politely, she says she is not interested in money. Then I remember that what I must say with this kind of person is, 'please'. 'Please, Miss Whittaker, please, I'm *desperate*, and I really can't come any other day.' The appointment is arranged.

Now it's merely a question of getting Shirley to let me have Hilary for the afternoon. Because I don't want Shirley to know. Lourdes is one thing, huge, institutional, traditional, respectable. Everybody tries Lourdes. You'd be amazed how many common-or-garden, middle-class protestants have been there with their chronic arthritis, low sperm counts, dyslexic children and miscellaneous cancers. Lourdes is respectable. But a faith-healer off the Fulham Road is something else altogether. The trouble being that the more I try to solve the problem, to save Hilary rather than just leave be, the more bizarre the gestures I make, so the closer Shirley believes I'm getting to doing something drastic.

A certain macabre suspicion has crept into our relationship. She keeps her eye on me.

'I just thought I'd take her off your back for an afternoon. Give you a chance to relax.'

Shirley is indeed worn out. Who wouldn't be? It's been a week of ear infection again. Hilary can't take regular antibiotics because of the additives they have. She is likewise allergic to the solution most drops come in.

'Of course if you don't want me to get close to my daughter . . .'

She concedes.

And as I prepare Hilary for the trip I sense again how right I am to insist on finding some kind of solution that will truly be a solution, on not accepting this miserable situation as permanent. For just getting a coat and hat on the girl is a hopeless, wearing, heartbreaking task. Her arms won't go in the holes. The elbows don't bend properly. She wriggles and moans, arching her little body fiercely, unnaturally, backwards, eyeballs rolling away so that the iris is almost gone.

I try so hard to be gentle. I force a hand into a sleeve. Then she scratches herself quite badly behind an ear. There's blood.

Shirley says I haven't the knack.

I say the girl's nails shouldn't be allowed to get so long. Briefly I reflect on the quite endless occasions for discord.

I carry her down the back steps to the garage tossed over my shoulder like a sack of potatoes. She has no muscle-tone. She can't cling to me like a normal child would. But sensing, from the changes in sound, smell and light, that we must be going out, she begins to gurgle happily. Then cries again as we go through the business of getting her into the car and into some kind of acceptable position on the car seat where I can strap her in. Leaving her crying, I hurry back to the house for nappies, creams, her special two-ton pushchair.

I tell Shirley I'm taking her to hear the band in St James's Park. It's a pleasant spring afternoon. Open air and music are two of the few things she is capable of enjoying, aren't they? Shirley is touched now and embraces me. We would both like not to argue, to be close. 'George,' she mutters. 'Thanks, really.'

In the car when I look in the mirror, my daughter's head is

lolling heavily to one side, a beatific smile on her face which gradually smooths out into sleep. At least I get the fun of the drive.

I suppose I'm expecting somebody thin, drawn, spiritual, mysterious, perhaps dressed in black. I have in mind a medium I saw on some up-market TV drama with dull, glazed, at once unseeing and all-seeing eyes. A make-up job probably. Instead, having humped the sleeping Hilary down a flight of cement steps and negotiated my way past a line of bins and assorted pots with geranium cuttings, I am greeted by a woman who surprises me by her likeness to my mother when she was younger. It is the florid, matronly wholesomeness of the round middle-aged face that strikes me, the clear, kind eyes.

'You must be Mr Crawley. Do come in. Is this your little daughter?'

Miss Whittaker's dumpy body is dressed cheaply and sensibly in patterned skirt and synthetic pink sweater. I am disappointed. Far from a mysterious place of healing, her flat might be any of the more middle-class variety one sees when visiting colleagues from work: stuffy, cleanly-kept, unexciting. Photographs of relatives and so on. Though plentiful flowers do give a sense of repose.

'Mrs Johnson told me about you.'

She wrinkles her forehead and frowns: 'Mrs Johnson? I've got a head like a sieve I'm afraid.'

'She had a bad back and . . .'

'Oh, yes, right. It's better now of course.'

'Yes, it is.'

'I am glad. And what can I do for you?'

Catching a faint twinkle in her clear eyes I realise that she is aware of, and rather amused by, my sense of disappointment. She is intelligent.

As I begin to mumble my story she walks me through to a small back bedroom where floral curtains and a mass of potted plants are allowing only a dim green light to filter onto spartan furnishings: divan bed, armchair, chair, bookcase. There is none of the religious bric-a-brac I had imagined. Not even the texts my mother invariably hangs on bedroom walls ('They shall rise up on wings as eagles: they shall run and not faint'). Perhaps it's not going to be the performance I expected.

'Ah, the girl. No, don't tell me anything, Mr Crawley. No medical details, please. It only interferes. Just lay her on the bed then, will you.'

Naturally as I try to slip her coat off, for the room is over-heated, Hilary wakes with a heart-stopping howl that freezes thought. Her mouth opens wide, wide, wide. She wails. Under my breath I involuntarily mutter, 'Bloody hell!' And immediately, startlingly, I sense that although it is surely impossible with the volume of that howling, Miss Whittaker has somehow heard me. I turn quickly to find her smiling at me with sympathy, but also with a certain sternness. Again I am reminded of my mother.

'You don't believe, do you, Mr Crawley?'

'No, I'm afraid I don't.'

'You don't believe I have any power.'

She talks sweetly without any hint of challenge.

'Well, I . . .'

And all the while I'm trying to stop poor bloody Hilary from rolling off the bed. She is unusually agitated.

'So may I ask why you came?'

With sudden and I know rude belligerence, I say, 'Why shouldn't I come? I've got nothing to lose.'

She doesn't react. On the contrary, there is something irritatingly demure about the way she stands with her fleshy white hands folded in front of her. 'I think I understand,' she says. 'In any event it surely doesn't help if you curse and swear over your child, does it?' She raises her eyebrows. We exchange a brief glance, during which I again have the impression that she is coolly aware of what I am thinking: that she is a pious fraud.

'Do you want me to undress her?' I ask. The child is crying softly now.

'No, no, you just relax and sit in the armchair for a little, will you?'

I had been afraid I might be asked to pray or something. She waits for me to move away and then goes to the bed and strokes Hilary's hair. Immediately the child quietens and begins to gurgle softly.

'What a pretty little girl,' Miss Whittaker murmurs. 'What a pretty pink ribbon Mummy has put in your hair. What pretty clothes. Someone's mummy and daddy think a lot of them, don't they? Someone's a very lucky little girl.'

Curiously, she is right. We do think a lot of her.

I sit in the chair watching the woman's squat back. Hilary is lying quite still and calm, despite the strange place, the strange voice. This is very unusual. A good sign. So, do I sense the faintest ray of hope? It's quickly quelled. How can this woman even know what's wrong with my daughter? There's nothing to be seen without taking her clothes off. She's not obviously spastic or mongoloid. The charlatan doesn't know what I brought her for.

Kneeling on a cushion, Miss Whittaker runs her small podgy hands the length of the child's body, letting them slide lightly over her clothes. Minutes pass. She has stopped talking now, her hands move back and forth, not hypnotically or even rhythmically, but more with a questing motion, stopping here and there, hovering, moving back, coming quietly to rest: on her head for a full minute, above her knees, her ankles, which below her socks, I know, are fierce with scars. Hilary lies still, eyes blindly open, breathing soft. She doesn't even move when a plump hand covers her face, gently pressing the eyelids. Leaning over her, Miss Whittaker blows very lightly on her forehead. Then repeats the whole rigmarole.

I watch, biting a nail. Fifteen minutes. It's hard keeping still frankly. I fidget. I feel tense. It's farcical. For of course, now I'm here, I don't expect anything. In the end I would have done a lot better by myself and Hilary if I'd gone to St James's Park. Shirley would think I'd lost my marbles.

Another ten minutes before at last Miss Whittaker rises slowly to her feet, then sits on the bed and strokes Hilary's hair in what is now an entirely normal way. Immediately the child begins to smile and gurgle again.

'Poor little lovey.' Then she turns to me. She says: 'Well, apart from some small irritation or infection which I may have been able to help, your child is really perfectly healthy, Mr Crawley, and beautifully, beautifully innocent. Don't you see how her smiles shine?'

What? Is the 'session' over? Is that her verdict? But she holds up a hand to stop my protest. 'As for the question of what she is, I mean the form in which she was sent into this world, I'm afraid it is far, far beyond my humble powers to alter that.'

After a moment's awkward silence in this dimly-lit room, I decide the best thing to do is cut my losses. Only £12.50 after all. A joke. I stand up to go, reaching for my wallet.

She smiles her sad smile, so similar to any sympathetic, middle-class smile an older woman might give you waiting in a long queue at supermarket or post office. She is still stroking Hilary's hair. For the first time, standing above her now as she moves her legs, crosses her ankles, I think of her as feminine, ample, faintly perfumed, a woman. They are always women. And she says calmly:

'Perhaps I could help you, though, Mr Crawley.'

'I'm sorry, I beg your pardon.'

'Perhaps I could help you more than your child.'

'Oh I'm fine.' Caught by surprise, I automatically assume my jocular office persona. 'As terminal patients go I mean.' I laugh falsely. I'm never ready for people's extraordinary presumption.

She raises her eyebrows. 'In some ways you may be less healthy than your daughter.'

'That,' I tell her emphatically, dropping any attempt at humour, 'is patently non-sense. Anyway, I'm in a hurry.'

'Of course, as you wish.' But then as I extract my wallet, she adds: 'It's just that you said you were desperate.'

'I am. For her.'

'And for yourself.'

'Only in so far as I find her suffering unbearable.'

'So perhaps I could help you with your desperation, help

136

you to bear it.' She works on me with her soft eyes the way certain women will.

'Frankly I'd say desperation was the only normal response to this situation. I shall be desperate while she is like she is. She is the cause, not a symptom. And that's that.'

Miss Whittaker sighs, faintest half-smile wrinkling the corners of a generous pale mouth. 'As you wish. Dear Hilary,' she says again as I struggle to get her into her coat.

At the door she declines payment with a simple shake of the head. She has exactly my mother's serene sad wistfulness. For Christ's fucking sake. I hate people who won't take the money you owe them.

And once in the car I go for the Fulham Road with a real vengeance. Only at the second or third lights do I remember I'd offered to take her to Richmond. Of course. Suddenly it's very important that I honour this promise. I don't want to be thought a shit. I am not. Quite the contrary. I swing the car through a U-turn, alarming the inevitable pensioner in his Morris 1100. But when I get back to Fernshaw Road no one answers the door. She has put two milk bottles out that I don't remember seeing before. I look up and down what is after all a fairly long street. Could she really have walked so far?

At the first newsagents I pick up a few bars of chocolate and feed myself quickly, heading for Battersea Park. Who knows if a band mightn't be playing there? In the mirror I can see poor Hilary's lolling head. My eyes fill with tears. It is this I can't stand. I would so dearly like to give my daughter some chocolate, to see her gobble it up greedily like I do. I would like to give her at least this small piggy pleasure: good thick foil-wrapped chocolate. But the sugar brings Hilary out in rashes that cover her whole body.

I shan't be going to any faith-healers again.

The Good Samaritan

January 1988. Hilary is five. Feeding her this morning, I thought: 'We get less change out of her than one would out of a three-week-old puppy.' I alternate between this ruthless realism and cloying sentimentality. The girl is so constipated that sometimes we have to hook a finger into her anus and lever the turds out. Shirley does this. I simply can't.

Travelling to work, I am fascinated by the truth that I am both seriously mentally disturbed and at the same time among the most conventional of commuters on the Northern Line; the soberly dressed junior director of a highly successful software company, personally responsible for a whole new concept of computer usage on small- to medium-size building sites. Forty grand. Saab Turbo. Walletful of plastic. On/off highly erotic affair with lovely marketing director, Marilyn.

But the *Telegraph* tells me that an Indian in Walsall has been arrested for the attempted murder of his five-year-old Downs syndrome son using poisonous mushrooms masked in a hot curry. I buy the *Telegraph* now, not just because it is generally free of the kind of social pieties one finds in the other 'serious' dailies, but mainly for the eye they have for these sort of stories. The paper comments briefly on the deplorable morals of some ethnic minorities who not only abort healthy foetuses for no other reason than that they're female, but have a quite horrific record as far as handicapped children are concerned. 'All too often the social services cover up such incidents out of a perverse inversion of race discrimination. In March 1986 a young black girl suffering from elephantiasis was burnt to death in a caravan in Brixton. The story was not . . .'

Fire. The idea suddenly comes to me. Cleansing fire.

If the cause were sufficiently disguised . . .

For a moment I am quite rapt by the beauty of this solution. Fire. Pushing my way through the crowd at Hammersmith with briefcase and squash racket before me, I am, as it were, enveloped in flames. I can really see myself doing it at last. This is actually possible.

But not in our beautiful Hampstead home.

For Mr Harcourt, I should have said, died last year, just as we were about to set off to Lourdes. Which is why in the end we never went. Being a profoundly lucky man he died suddenly: heart attack on the john, in company of the *FT*. In any event, we called off the trip to Lourdes for the various solemnities, quickly followed by the sharing of the spoils, which in this case, fortunately, were considerable indeed. Of course, the taxman took his whack, but what was left, in *both* our names I was relieved to see, allowed us to move up into the three-hundred-grand property bracket. Gainsborough Gardens, a gorgeous close a stone's throw from the Heath and no more than five minutes from the tube.

I'm not going to burn that place down.

'Unless somehow,' I'm saying to myself on the return journey of that same day, 'it's the sacrifice required of me.'

What a strange thought! Much easier surely, just to refuse her oxygen when she has one of her respiratory problems. How could they ever really know I'd done it on purpose.

But staring at my curiously double image in the carriage window, I remember an incident of a few weeks ago which made a big impression on me. I'd stopped to fill up on the Finchley Road and after paying, as I was walking to my car, somebody on the road hit a cat. The animal wasn't dead. Using just its front paws and squawking fearfully it dragged itself toward me in spastic jerks across a patch of pavement. With the winter evening's yellow sodium light, its mutilation was garishly lit. Its back haunches had been completely crushed into a pulp of black fur and blood. Its wild howls were attracting the attention of passers by. Then, unable to pull itself further, it lay and writhed. Clearly the one thing to do to this cat was to get a brick, or even the jack from the boot, and put it out of its misery as soon as possible. Yet nobody did this. Not I, nor the home-going secretaries, executives, workers. Nobody had sufficient compassion or courage to dirty their hands with a liberating violence, to bring down the brick, the jack on this poor animal's skull. Nor did anybody want to talk about it. They hurried by silently, not stopping. Perhaps, you could suppose, if it had been a question of playing Good Samaritan, of saving an animal with glass in its paw, a cut on its haunch, perhaps somebody would have stopped. For that is something entirely different and infinitely easier. But what was needed here was a savage *coup de grâce*. And for maybe two or three minutes I hesitated, staring at this shrieking cat. Then got into the Saab and drove away.

House or no house, the advantage of the fire is that I would not need to be in the same room as her. I would not have to see her clawing for breath.

But what decides me in the end is Peggy's abortion. We have been seeing Peggy and Charles regularly for a couple of years now. Really, they are our only visitors. Shirley did go through a period of trying to contact and make friends with other couples with handicapped children, and we would drive out to meet them some evenings or Saturday afternoons. One does these things, looking for reassurance, I suppose, others in the same boat. But it was too depressing. One's own handicapped child is bad enough, but the deformities and spastic contortions of a stockbroker's boy in Walthamstow, a railway worker's teenage daughter in Hounslow are too appalling. And far, far from reassuring. Merely a reminder in fact of how lost and wave-tossed the shared boat is. Somehow the more these people insisted on the little progresses, the tiny achievements of their doomed offspring, the more obstinately cheerful they were, showing you family photos in fields of flowers, so the worse, at least for me, the whole scenario became. Until, with the reasonable excuse that we were only depressing ourselves, I managed to put an end to this interlude. Shirley offered no resistance. She is not quite at my mother's level of martyrdom yet. In fact we will have these moments, sitting on the sofa for example, watching the box, when our fingers will meet, involuntarily it seems, and some kind of communication, of affection will pass between us.

We haven't made love for more than five years.

Shirley has confiscated and burnt my euthanasia scrapbook. Though I don't generally go in for hocus pocus, I find the fact that she *burnt* it excitingly symbolic. Anyway, I shan't be collecting any more such articles now. I sense the need for them is over.

Although never exactly assiduous, all our old regular friends, Gregory and Jill and Shirley's one-time school colleagues, have completely dropped off. They find it too hard to handle. Shirley has her church friends of course, but she generally sees them in the morning or afternoon when I'm at work, or at Wednesday evening choir practice or after Sunday Morning Service. So our paths don't cross. Anyway I have no desire to see them. Their determined niceness grates on me, reminds me of Mother humming 'Count your blessings', under an umbrella on Park Royal Road with an empty purse in her threadbare pocket. There is a primal anguish behind it all for me, dating back I sometimes wonder, to some experience I can't even remember. I dream my dreams of mutilation.

But we do see Charles and Peggy. They come over once, twice, even three times a week, eat with us, talk, argue. They always come together because they are sharing a house he has persuaded his buddies in Camden Council Housing Authority to let Peggy have, pending demolition. This is a wangle I'm sure. They've had the place more than a year now and there's no sign of the bulldozers. Meanwhile, God knows in what investments Charles has sunk the hundred and fifty-odd grand he got from Daddy-oh. In British Airports, I wouldn't be surprised. Nothing would surprise me.

I didn't realise they were lovers at first. Why? Because Peggy has always enthused over her lovers, always pronounced herself everlastingly in love with them. Because, being our brother and sister, they have a good excuse for arriving together. Because Charles never shows a shred of fatherliness toward the exhaustingly exuberant Freddie. And because I always suspected he was queer.

'Peggy mentioned it,' Shirley tells me one day.

'Mentioned it!'

'She was very offhand.'

'Wonders will never cease.'

'I was thinking, probably that's why he became so assiduous about visiting us in the first place. To see her.'

I reflect on this.

'They don't show any affection together. Why don't they act like a couple?'

'The amazing thing about you,' Shirley says, 'is that for all your super logic and supposed modernity, you're so incredibly traditional.'

'Sorry, I just thought it was common sense. You're lovers, you live together, you may as well act like a couple.'

'Why don't you just accept that people are different. You got angry with her when she was naïve, now maybe she's being less so.'

But although in some obscure way I disapprove of Charles and Peggy, I do enjoy their visits. Discussing things between four people they seem manageable, whereas on one's own, or alone with Shirley, hysteria is always just around the corner.

'Now the girl's five,' Charles tells us this evening, 'you're due for nappy relief, since a normal child would now be out of nappies.'

'Oh yes?' Shirley asks chattily. 'What do we have to do?'

Charles begins to describe the bureaucratic procedure. He obviously enjoys this. His voice is quick, incisive, very faintly patronising in a teacherly sort of way. As he speaks, lean and sinewy, I watch how his thin fingers twine and untwine around a tumbler. His Adam's apple is also jerkily mobile.

'A wonder they haven't cut it,' Peggy remarks. She is helping Frederick with a jigsaw puzzle of the Changing of the Guard.

'No, there's no actual means test *per se*,' Charles reassures.

'More to the point they need a letter from your GP to the effect that the child really is incontinent.'

'Fair enough. After all, they're eight quid a box,' Shirley says, 'and it's only paper and a bit of plastic in the end.'

'You know you can't use them at all in Washington State,' Peggy informs. 'Anti-ecological.'

'Then you present proof of purchase and you get the cash.'

I remark that eight quid, what, a week, isn't going to change our lives in any major way, is it? It hardly seems worth the time in the queue. In fact – and I make the mistake of getting drawn into an old argument – the whole point about state help, or any such sops of this kind, is that they merely draw your attention away from the real issue while you waste your time picking up crumbs.

'And what is the real issue?' Charles asks sharply.

'That this is *our* problem. Our huge problem, and we're stuck with it. There is no imaginable help that could really amount to anything or significantly change our lives.'

'Well, obviously it's useful for the less well-off,' Charles says, faintly offended by my lack of interest, 'which is why the government's no doubt trying to cut it.'

'But we're not less well off, we're rich. I'm on forty-plus grand. If I don't pick it up there'll be more for someone else.'

'No, if people don't pick it up, the government'll say they don't need it and remove it all together.'

Looking away from me to inspect a ladder on dark tights, Shirley says: 'George is just lamenting the absence of state assisted abortion post birth.' She looks up with her little smile. '*N'est-ce-pas?*'

I shrug my shoulders. We're old campaigners now. I don't think either of us is capable of shocking the other any more. 'Abortion certainly solves a problem in a way a few quid for nappies doesn't.'

Then before Charles can stop her, Peggy says simply: 'I'm going to have to have an abortion. Next week.' And very matter of fact, she explains that she is pregnant by Charles (he fidgets fiercely, pushes thumb and forefinger around his teeth), but that he doesn't want the child. Anyway, she already has Freddy and that's quite enough for anyone the way men come and go. She doesn't seem to be saying this as an attack on Charles, or even as an expression of reproach.

Why am I so stunned? It is the ease with which my sister handles these decisions, the lack of any hint of guilt.

'She insisted,' Charles says, 'on using the Okino Knauss method.'

Peggy laughs: 'Rhythm and blues! In that order. Still, I just can't afford another.'

Later, when they have gone, I watch Shirley liquidising meat to store away in little tubs in the freezer for all Hilary's meals for the week to come. She follows an intense routine now of keeping house and feeding Hilary. She is always doing something, locked into some procedure.

'What do you make of that?'

She shrugs her shoulders. 'Probably they're afraid it'll be like Hilary.'

'But we asked, on her behalf, don't you remember. It was one of the first things I did. And the specialist said how unlikely it was and that anyway they can test for it now they know it's a possibility.'

Shirley doesn't seem interested.

'The child is probably perfectly healthy,' I insist.

'So maybe it is.'

Obliquely I say: 'Soon they'll be able to keep foetuses alive as soon as the cells meet. Will they still let people abort them?'

As if she were another part of my own mind, she says: 'No, at that point, they'll tell you you can kill anybody who's helpless and inconvenient.'

'But why didn't she use contraceptives, for heaven's sake?'

Shirley's working fast, slicing some stewing meat into manageable chunks. Her once finely tapered pale fingers are growing rough and red, like Mother's.

'We all have our fixations. She's into Buddhism, natural foods, natural body functions, no contraceptives. Charles is into politics, his career, he doesn't want a kid he would have to feel responsible for. Probably he's quite right.'

'And you?' I ask with the husky tenderness that will sometimes spring up unexpected as a wild flower on the roughest terrain. 'Don't you think life should have a certain grace, Shirley?'

'Leave be, George,' she says. 'Please, please, please leave be.'

Foul Medicine

I'm not a pig. In an attempt to recapture something of my relationship with Shirley I decide on a vasectomy, let's see if we can't get back to lovemaking. She says: 'I'll have forgotten how to do it. I can't quite see why we ever bothered, it's so much more hygienic without it.' Though a week or so before the op she hugs me from behind, squeezes my crotch, and murmurs: 'I can't wait, if you knew how much I want you and want you.'

Since I'm determined no one at the office should know about the whole thing, I take a fortnight's holiday during which time I arrange for the operation to be done privately in the London Clinic in Harley Street. Typically, Shirley informs my mother without first conferring with me, hence the day after the op, there she is at my bedside in her ancient black coat with the fake once-white fur inside the collar. The strap of her blue handbag, doubtless full of used paper handkerchiefs, is held on by a heavy duty safety pin.

My mother. She sold Gorst Road to the first buyer and then instead of getting a smaller place for herself and keeping the remaining cash for Grandfather's expenses, she went and put the whole lot in Barclays for him with a standing order to pay the home ('it's his money, love,'), renting herself the most miserable terraced house in derelict black Irish Cricklewood. Apparently through friends! It was a show of independence that took me by surprise, since I'd imagined she'd leave the whole property side of things to me. As it was she didn't even ask my advice. We have scarcely seen each other since Shirley's 'conversion'.

Shirley said: 'Why didn't she stay in Park Royal. She's

been there all her life. She'll be lost in a new neighbourhood at her age.' But although she knew no one in Cricklewood on arrival, Mother very quickly gathered the regular army of walking wounded about her. Indeed her 'ministry' is obviously flourishing now Grandfather is at last out of the way. People don't have to pass his scornful cerberian gaze to reach the prayerfulness of her bedroom. So perhaps all things do work together for good for those that love God: my beating him up promoted her ministry, saved souls even.

She stands over my hospital bed the morning after my vasectomy, plastic shopping bag under her arm. We are embarrassed, but she tries to jolly her way over this.

'How are you, love? Everything all right?'

Actually I've got quite a lot of pain. It was a more serious business than I expected.

She has brought grapes. Her face, though shiny and lumpy, radiates unshakeable kindness. We chat. She has been up to see Shirley. In my absence obviously. Over sixty now, she travels free on the buses. It's quite a boon. She feels free to travel in a way she didn't just a year ago. And isn't Hilary coming on, certainly sitting up a lot straighter.

I say: 'You don't notice when you're with her all the time.'

I ask her if she knew about Peggy. And immediately regret it. But I don't want to be the only one who's let her down.

'She told me.'

Peggy would of course. Without thinking probably.

For a moment we are both silent in this tiny private bedroom I have paid through the nose for. The fittings don't look much better than National Health frankly.

Why did I bother trying to hurt her? Surely some resolution, some accommodation can be reached at some point.

She must be thinking the same thing, because she suddenly says, lower lip trembling like a child's: 'Can't we put all that nasty business behind us, George? Can't we?'

The direct appeal catches me by surprise.

She says: 'It was unfortunate Shirley confessed to me of

147

all people, and in front of you, but I could hardly refuse to hear her, poor girl, could I, the state she was in.'

How clever my mother is. She has brought me to tears. We are embracing.

'At least we can be good friends,' she murmurs, with a catch in her voice.

Then she sits down and tells me how awkward Grand-father's being, refusing to obey any of the rules in the home and even biting one of the nurses. It's his ninetieth birthday next week. The inmates will be having a little party. Perhaps I'd like to come. And then the Lord has been so good to her because her next door neighbour but one commutes regularly to Kilburn where the home is and so frequently gives her a lift back in the evening. Also there is a delightful girl from the church who may be going to rent her spare bedroom, which would be so nice.

There is always that faint persuasion in her voice, she can never let go, pleading with her son to believe that the Lord has indeed been involved in the daily itinerary of her neighbour, the housing needs of the Methodist girl; pleading with me to accept my martyrdom and join her on the way to heaven.

Shortly after she goes, Marilyn phones. 'Can't wait to have you without your sou'wester on,' she says.

But I know I won't be going to see Marilyn again. My strategy is complete at last. I was always a monogamist at heart.

For the second week of my fortnight's break we've lined up a cottage in Suffolk, for holiday and, hopefully, celebratory hanky panky, if not actually lovemaking. Our first real holiday, as it happens, since Hilary's conception nearly six years (centuries?) before. But when I come out of hospital, feeling pretty damn cool and relaxed actually, after four whole days on my back, the child has fallen ill again.

She has an acute kidney infection (perhaps like the George of *Three Men in a Boat*, the only thing she'll never have is housemaid's knee). And of course she always suffers severe side effects from whatever drug we give her. Shirley meets me sleepless and speechless at our rather fine old wistaria-framed door as I return in a cab. The doctor wanted to put the girl in hospital, but Shirley has refused. I know there is no point in commenting on this, just as there is no point in remarking on the fact that we could easily afford to have a nurse in to do a few nights. Shirley must look after the girl herself. Because I think in a curious way she is embarrassed for Hilary with strangers. She doesn't want to sense other people's objective eyes coldly weighing up the truth of the situation. On her own she can nurse her illusions – or perhaps that is ungenerous, perhaps what I should say is, the choices she has made. She doesn't want to hear them challenged by some kind, efficient girl. For my own part, of course, there is nothing more frustrating than having so much money at last after years of work and not being allowed to buy a little pleasure with it.

Hilary is in severe pain. Naturally, through the long nights and days that follow my return there will be no question of trying out my vasectomy. Though one evening Shirley does cling tight to me a moment in bed. She murmurs: 'You know what I can't believe about you, George.' 'What?' 'That deep down, after all your huffing and puffing and playing tough, you're really a good man.'

I make no comment.

'I'm glad you made up with your mother. I'll have her over tomorrow to help if she's free.'

Obviously everything gets chatted about behind my back. Fair enough I suppose. I never really imagined otherwise.

'I don't even really mind about this woman you've got at work. I understand the pressure you must have been under.'

'What?'

A desperate half hour then trying to persuade her that all that's over, that I only saw her once or twice, that I never really cared for her, etc., etc. And how did she find out, anyway? How, how, how? Shirley insists she doesn't care. After all, she's been unfaithful in her time. I insist that she should, she must care, it was a terrible thing for me to do, I want her to care, and I'm sorry, truly I am; that was the whole reasoning behind the vasectomy after all, to get back to her and to family life after this second derailment. Which would never have happened had it not been for Hilary.

In the end, after maybe an hour's persuasion I actually manage to get her involved in something resembling foreplay, kissing, fondling, albeit somewhat listlessly, when Hilary's harsh cries interrupt us from the next room.

I offer to go since I'm on holiday. Anyway, there's guilt to assuage. I pad down the landing.

The baby's room has a red nightlight. It's full of cuddly toys which Hilary has at last learnt to hold to herself and presumably draw some comfort from. The little girl is twisting and turning in her cot, buckled up with stomach pains. I pick her up. Not without some effort given the size she is now. She recognises me at once and whimpers. I push my cheek against hers on the side where the head lolls. Her skin, poor girl, is dry and burning. She relaxes a little, then doubles up with pain again. Her eyes screw tight. Since it's impossible to sit her on one's knee – she just collapses – I put her into a little tipped-back bucketseat kind of thing that we had cut for her from a huge cube of rigid foam rubber. This more or less immobilises her while keeping her sufficiently upright to take a few spoonfuls of medicine.

I give her a specially made up additive-free antibiotic and a sedative in heavy syrup. The antibiotic tastes foul and she refuses to open her mouth. I trick her by dipping my finger in the sedative syrup and smearing it lightly on her plump, child's lips. She has the features of a five-year-old but utterly blank. Sometimes I force myself to use words like gormless, to remember what the hard world will think of her, how they will laugh, as once long ago my friends would laugh at Aunt Mavis. The coral lips are delicate though and faintly rubbery under my finger.

She falls for the syrup trick and opens her mouth. As soon as the spoon of foul-tasting medicine is in, I force the mouth shut to prevent her from spitting the stuff out. I manage to do this quite gently really. Firmly. Without frightening her. I'm not bad as a nurse. The only problem then is convincing her that the syrup to follow really is syrup. In the end I have to press thumb and forefinger into her cheeks to force open the mouth. As soon as she gets the whole spoon of syrup I can give her two, three, four more spoonfuls. Double the maximum dose. From small red-rimmed brown eyes, she looks, or gives the impression of looking, in my direction, and there is a hint of appreciation. So that I sense how much within my power she is, her feverish infant body in that foam rubber chair we thought was such a clever idea.

For I could keep spooning and spooning this whole bottle of sedative, couldn't I? Her mouth is open, eager. So why don't I? Why not? Because I know that Shirley would see. Because I reason that the way they measure out these drugs it wouldn't quite kill her anyway. Because it's not the solution I've settled on and I simply can't face reopening the whole discussion. Yet in the quiet of her little nursery room, with its red light warm on walls and blankets, on the Beatrix Potter frieze and on the shambles of soft toys people like my mother insist on buying for her as if she were capable of distinguishing one from another – in this cosy atmosphere smelling of cream and talcum and warm breath, I feel that this would be an acceptable, a humane way to do it. If only society would sanction it. If only everybody would say, yes, George, we forgive you, George, you are right, George, go ahead, kill your dragon, save your damsel (for I do love her). Yes, here and now. This would be the way. Spooning sedative to the child as she senses my friendly presence and enjoys one of her few sensual luxuries, the rich cloying sweetness of that syrup.

Are those red little eyes really looking at me? Is she asking me to do it?

But of course she can have no concept of such things. All she knows is her pain, her comforts.

She begins to whine and wriggle again. I lay her down and sing to her. Nursery rhymes. Christmas carols. I sing them with expression as if I meant them. I even sing, why I don't know, 'Rock of ages cleft for me', insisting on the words of the last verse (When I soar through tracts unknown/See thee on thy judgement throne . . .). I keep it up for half an hour, wondering how Shirley will rate this virtuoso performance on the domestic contribution scales. Will Marilyn be forgotten? Will I ever get a blowjob again? Finally I pull off the miracle and my little girl falls into an uneasy sleep. Feeling really pretty proud, I pad back to our bedroom, but Shirley is snoring soundly. Fair enough, she does have a filthy cold. I slip downstairs, pour myself a generous Glenfiddich and watch a European football match in which a Scottish team is soundly beaten.

Vasectomy Ball

Our tenth wedding anniversary, I think, should be excuse enough for a party, but Shirley says wrily, 'Hardly an occasion for celebration.' She's not really objecting, though. It's just that she never expected the idea of a party to come from me.

'If you look at it as a life sentence,' I suggest, 'let's say we're celebrating completion of the first quarter. Why not?'

I'm straightening my tie. She's copying things down from a recipe to complete a shopping list, writing rapidly, a sliver of tongue between her teeth as so often when she concentrates. Now she looks up.

'You're not serious, are you?' She laughs. 'Okay. I'm game. We can call it the Vasectomy Ball.'

Because yesterday we finally made love. And again this morning. Hence the pleasant atmosphere. I choose my moments.

I tell her: 'You don't want to spread that kind of news about, sweetheart, the phone'll never stop ringing.'

Again she laughs. Then wrinkles her nose. She really doesn't seem to care terribly much about my faithfulness or otherwise. In many ways she is more independent of me than I of her. I can't really decide whether this is a good thing or not. I don't want to feel free to do what I choose. I want her to want all or nothing, like me. Perhaps when she no longer has the child to exhaust all her energies . . .

Come the evening of that same day and she is positively enthusing about it – our Tenth Anniversary Party. A grand affair. In the space of a day the idea has taken on a milestone symbolism. George and Shirley back on the rails.

'You see,' she says happily, as we draw up the guest list. 'There's no reason why Hilary should prevent us from having a good time. It's all in your mind.'

The girl is half sitting, half lying in her lap. At five and a half she has begun to chant the first ma-ma-ma's and da-da-da's that most babies start at six months. Shirley is very excited about this, though there is no sign of the sounds being referred to anything or anyone in particular. The little girl smiles continuously this evening from inside the frame of her gloriously thick chestnut hair which Shirley keeps brilliantly washed and brushed. Her only real asset, it picks up faint hints and depths from the discrete wall lighting which proved such a wise and fashionable choice. When tickled under her tubby chin, she giggles. She hasn't been ill for upwards of a fortnight now, and since a dietician suggested we substitute cow's milk with goat's, she has definitely been less irritated and irritable.

These are the blessings Shirley counts with a religious mathematics she might have learnt from my mother, i.e. add this hundredth to that thousandth, multiply by whatever crumb or fragment is available and then lift to the power of a small sop and somehow you can cancel out negative figures with untold noughts after them.

'No reason at all,' Shirley goes on, kissing the child's fat cheeks as I scribble out the names. 'We should have started doing this ages ago. I mean, if we can't go out, obviously we'll have to have people come here. And if we don't invite them they're not going to come, are they?'

I don't remark that they used to invite themselves. Instead I say: 'I haven't exactly been preventing you from inviting them, have I?'

'No, but you're such a monster of purpose, always working or reading medical journals or planning trips to consultants. It's as if you were always putting off living to some distant date when you'll have sorted everything out.' She lays a hand on the inside of my leg and looks into my eyes. 'I'm glad you're beginning to let be at last. If you don't insist on its being a tragedy then it isn't.'

The touch has a definite promise of sex.

She giggles. 'Perhaps it's to do with the op. Less hormones about or something. You're mellowing out.'

I haven't seen her so silly and girlish in years, though the silver strands are daily thickening in her once copper hair.

'We'll invite everybody,' she says. 'Even if we haven't seen them in years and years. We can clear the lounge and dining room for dancing and set out a big buffet in the kitchen and breakfast room. How much money can we afford to spend?'

'Anything. Doesn't matter. No object.'

'Great, now, let's see . . .'

But what is George Crawley really thinking inside the dark lumpy 900ccs or so which is his brain, which is me? Obviously I am feeling terribly tender toward my suddenly excited, though definitely ageing wife. I am thinking how smart I've been to renew our relationship before the great event, to have her feel I'm on her side at last. And I'm genuinely heartened by the thought that after all we've been through this renewal can still occur and be so warm and genuine. I'm thinking that in a way I'm doing this for her sake even more than mine. But at the same time I am wondering if perhaps she isn't right, could she be?, if perhaps we mightn't be happy like this, if I shouldn't have let be ages ago, if I oughtn't to give the whole thing up and just enjoy the incongruous adventure of hosting a party. Suddenly surprising myself with all these heterogeneous thoughts, I shake my head to chase them all away. They rise and flutter like birds surprised by gunshot, leaving nothing behind. I wonder, where is my identity in all this chaos of feeling and reflection? Who am I? All I can sense is a feverish darkness gathered around an even darker purpose. I have given myself to the decision now. It won't be reconsidered.

'And for booze? Couple of hundred quid cover it do you think? Er, Earth to George, come in please. The booze. How much?'

'Oh.' In a daze, I say, 'The more the merrier.'

Another thought wings across the dark night sky of my spirit: the more booze, the faster the place'll go up in smoke.

Three weeks on; D-Day minus five days. I am now absolutely determined that the day after, Sunday the tenth, I shall feel only regret for my beautiful home, its three reception rooms, four bedrooms, delightful conservatory and garden (in the meantime I have checked that the insurance is more or less adequate; could have been better but one can't alter it now). I shan't fear detection, for of course I have planned the thing so well, and from the forensic point of view my tracks will be perfectly covered. Clearing the dining room to dance is going to mean cramming four highly inflammable armchairs into my little study, which, as fortune would have it, is directly below Hilary's room with only plaster and timber between. Ten minutes, max fifteen. All things work together for good . . .

For it will be an act of goodness, the first time I will have channelled everything that I know is abrasive and unpleasant in my character into a gesture of love greater and more healthy than anything my mother or Shirley with their interminable self-sacrifice could manage. I will have the courage of my convictions.

I Think of Us
Beginning Afresh

The most elementary secret to a successfully disguised arson is that the fire must have only one focal point. So far so good.

My mother is the first to arrive, bringing Frederick who she has been looking after for the day. She has construed her invitation, though this has never been asked, as a request for help and babysitting, and thus arrives early to give Shirley a hand with the food and with Hilary. Although she no doubt disapproves of the regiment of glinting bottles marshalled end to end of the sideboard, she is clearly glad that we are celebrating our tenth anniversary; no doubt she sees it as a kind of triumph over evil, a sign that our marriage is healthy again, and she mucks in, jollily washing saucepans.

Frederick, sensing excitement in the air, becomes a Japanese robot and struts about, hissing destructive laser sounds. He paces mechanically round and round Hilary who lies on her foam rubber mattress in the huge lounge now cleared for dancing. She wriggles wildly from side to side following the direction of his laser fire as best she can, her oddly flat face smiling blindly, unaware he is shooting her.

When she goes to bed, the foam mattress will go in the study room to make way for the dancing. I have already made sure that a huge pile of mags and newspapers are stacked on one of the armchairs.

Not to put too fine a point on it, I've been shitting a lot this afternoon, as was to be expected I'm afraid. Unpleasant, hot, acidic shits that leave your anus burning. I've got some good cream for it though. In the bathroom I run my fingers regretfully over silk-finish, coffee-coloured Italian tiles.

Opening the window I look out at a broad stretch of garden to the side of the house. A blackbird is hopping in the grass. There are roses. The air is sweet, soft. Toward the Heath, and this is always a symbol of joy for me, swallows are diving and wheeling in the warm twilight. Eating their prey alive of course. Though as a child I believed they just whirled about for fun.

Which reminds me, I must open the window in the study, make sure there's some oxygen about. Some weeks ago, complaining of Hilary's racket while I was debugging a program, I got Shirley to buy some strips of foam insulant to put round the door. No one will smell anything until it's roaring.

Coming down the stairs, I let my feet feel the fibrous sponginess of expensive pile carpet. My hand lingers on the polished wooden banister. Illuminating the red and gold wallpaper up the hallway are two light fittings with elaborate Venetian glass which Shirley bought from a shop in Belgravia. It annoys me that Mother never expresses any real admiration for this house, anything beyond, 'what big rooms, what a huge garden, it must be a nightmare keeping it tidy', etc. etc. If she were to show any desire to come and live here, instead of endlessly singing the praises of her Cricklewood shoebox, I would be glad to have her. I'm not in the business of bearing grudges.

And in fact I meet my mother going back to the kitchen. We hug warmly.

Almost seven o'clock. The kitchen and breakfast room are lined with tables draped with white cloths and laden with the kind of goodies we certainly never ate in Park Royal. The floor in the breakfast room is a dark herringbone parquet with two small Persian rugs. In the kitchen we have pearl grey polished granite tiles (not as expensive as you'd think).

What a long way I've come. And not all thanks to Shirley either (it was me, for example, chose the Regency dresser she loves so much). What a long way, just to find ourselves imprisoned by the life sentence Hilary is.

Shirley pulls a child's red plastic bowl from the fridge.

'I'll feed Hilary,' I offer.

'Oh thanks. I'll just heat it up a minute.'

The electronic bleeping of the microwave.

I refuse to go to the john again. Just ignore it, clench.

'Okay. Check it isn't too hot.'

To start the thing I shall use a cigarette smoked almost to the stub. I shall place it down the side of what, according to a government warning pamphlet found in Central Finchley library, should be our most inflammable armchair where I will have spilt/poured a full tumbler of whisky just a few minutes before. The armchair I have forced half under my desk and on the surface of the desk is a nearly full ashtray which I will tip over the chair as soon as the flames begin. This will thus seem, I trust, to those who sift through the ashes, to have been the little mishap that set the whole thing going: a jacket flap, or dress catches that ashtray as someone leaves the room, they don't wait to hear it fall and anyway it would be almost inaudible on the soft whisky-wet upholstery of the chair; in a few minutes the room is in flames.

I have made no attempt to salvage anything from this lovely little study room with its wood-panelled walls. Not my precious library of floppies with some of my best ideas for new software, not my IBM 8000 with expanded RAM. Not even our wedding photos in the bookcase. I feel quite glad to make these sacrifices, to lose things that are both valuable and precious. I think of us beginning afresh with the insurance money and a new house, and no Hilary. How free and happy we will be at last.

It would be dangerous to be seen to have squirrelled things away.

Forcing the girl into her special high chair, always a struggle, I almost burst out laughing: 'Too bad Grandad couldn't be here,' I shout to my mother as she clatters the vacuum cleaner back into the cupboard. 'He'd have a heart attack seeing all that booze.'

Mother doesn't like even the word, 'booze'.

'Poor old soul,' she says. 'If only he'd agree to have his teeth done it would be something.'

'Might be worse when he bit the nurses though.'

Both he and Hilary bite the hands that feed them.

'Poor old soul,' Mother says again, as if this were some kind of incantation. She will not think badly. Often I feel I've had to do the job for both of us.

I stir the food in its microwave dish and blow on it. Hilary is held upright by two strong waist bands and two rigid, vertical cushions either side of her head. Her face is at the same level as mine as I sit to feed her and she opens her mouth in anticipation. A few of Shirley's church friends have arrived, bringing more food, and somebody now puts Strauss's waltzes on, very loud. Hilary is suddenly so excited she bangs down her wrist in the dish, splattering chunks of ham and spaghetti rings, laughing furiously. The kind of thing that usually has me cursing with frustration (my trousers are splattered). But I'm cool tonight. We're on the home straight.

Then it vaguely occurs to me, is this what being mad is like? I aim a spoon into the glistening pink wetness of gums and lips. Her head waves perilously.

'Would you like an aperitif, sir?'

It's Shirley coming up behind me in excellent mood with a tray of chilled white wine.

It will look odd if I don't act merry and do some drinking. The party was my idea, wasn't it? Though I'll have to keep a clear head. The most important thing to remember is, since Frederick is to be put to bed in the spare bedroom, I shall have to get up there pretty smartly. But in a way that is part of the plan. I am hardly likely to forget.

And no, I will not go to the bathroom again.

The Romantic Fort

I always find parties of this kind in friends' houses somewhat
dull. Okay, you have a lot to eat, a lot to drink, that can be
nice, and maybe you manage to brush thighs, bump arses
with some pretty women jiving about the furniture. But
mostly you just find yourself sitting on the stairs with a plate
of sausage rolls, trapped into conversations so irretrievably
humdrum that even an argument with one's wife would be
exciting by comparison; this between getting up every couple
of minutes to let somebody climb upstairs to the loo. At
best you might find another man reasonably intelligent and
sufficiently interested in your own line of business to share
a bottle of whisky with till it's time to go home.

Which is why we've never had a party before, I suppose.
I remember Shirley was very eager to have a housewarming
do years ago when we moved into the Hendon place. 'Parties
are for fun,' she said. 'You're the one who's always saying he
wants to have a good time.'

And it's true. Parties are for fun. But the only people who
really seem to have any are the ones who break through
all inhibitions and get into snogging and petting and even
bonking people they've never met before. Those are the kind
who have fun. And the fact is that much as I envy them, I
would never be so much of a beast as to do stuff like that
with my wife around, or even amongst people who know
her. Often, I'm afraid, one must come to the conclusion that
one's inhibitions are the best part about one.

Other people are different of course. Some are quite shame-
less and have always done exactly what they want when they
want. So it is that towards midnight, my chosen hour for

the sale of my soul, I will slip discreetly out into the hall away from the guests in lounge and breakfast room, down the passage, through the cloakroom to the study, a lighted cigarette between the fingers of one hand, a big tumbler of whisky in the other, only to find Gregory and Peggy sprawled across two armchairs, more or less humping each other.

Why didn't I lock the door, for Christ's sake?

It's an odd party because we've invited such a mix of guests, many of whom we haven't seen for so long we can barely remember what they look like. We sent out sixty odd invitations but have no idea how many people are actually going to come. Twenty? A hundred? The invitations said eight thirty, but by nine only Shirley's friends from the choir have arrived, well-behaved, carefully-dressed people happy to drink a glass of white wine, eat snacks and speculate about their dictatorial organist/choirmaster's private life. The women take it in turns to hold Hilary in their arms and say how well she is looking. One, in a strapless black velvet outfit, looks just the kind decked out for pleasure she won't have. I can't help noticing her thin knees and calves and thinking of Marilyn.

Peggy phones to say she'll be late and can we put Frederick to bed or he'll become a monster. 'Grandma'll read you a story,' I tell him, thinking to kill two birds with one stone, have both of them out of the way. For Mother, after barely a glass of Soave, can be heard fervently praising the Lord in conversation with a plain weasily little man with his arm in a sling.

'I don't want Grandma to read a story. I want to stay downstairs. Five minutes, Uncle George.'

'Your mummy said bed.'

'Then you read, Uncle, I want you to read.'

He says this because he thinks I'll refuse. He's a sharp little lad with whom I feel a certain affinity. But as it happens I'm quite glad to be out of the fray for a while.

I take him upstairs, make him clean his teeth and sort through the kiddies' books people have occasionally given us, not realising Hilary will never be able to understand them. What would he like? Tom Thumb? He says the giant scares him. Eating the children. But it's only stalling. Nothing would scare Frederick. I tell him it's only pretend, there are no giants, nobody eats children. But I agree to dig out the Ugly Duckling instead. Where unfortunately, I reflect as I read, it is the welcome transformation that doesn't convince.

I kiss my nephew goodnight. Having got the door closed, I take the opportunity to change my soiled trousers and, before going downstairs again, size myself up in our wardrobe mirror. Five-ten. Blond. Pale-skinned, straight-nosed, clear eyes. Perhaps a little serious-looking, but certainly nothing loony about me. In the end, if I have to insist before a court of law on any one thing, it will be my complete normality, my modernity. Show me, I'll say to the jury, just one, just one part of my overall vision which is out of line with the dominant social philosophy in England today. I bet you can't. I just bet. But watching myself in the mirror I can see the tension about teeth and jaws. I have big jaw muscles.

Hearing noises at the top of the stairs I walk down the long landing to the other bathroom where Mother is struggling to change a particularly dirty nappy before putting Hilary to bed. I take over, for the girl's heavy and helpless and needs washing. I work quickly and efficiently and, though I say it myself, gently. Hilary always rouses a quite terrible gentleness in me. I wipe carefully inside the folds of skin around the pale warm split bun of her crotch. And talc generously.

At a certain point, my mother touches my shoulder and smiles at me with a bright winsome look. 'I think you're magnificent with the girl.' For some reason she says it in a whisper. Then in her normal voice. 'I'll put her to bed now. You go down and talk to your guests. It's your party.'

This is a little annoying because I had meant to give Hilary a very heavy dose of Calpol to make sure she won't wake and attract attention during the evening. As Mother walks off with the girl along the landing, she is already humming mournful hymn tunes which she presumably imagines are soporific. And indeed they are.

Downstairs I pin a little notice to the first column of the bannister. 'Use downstairs loo: don't want to wake kids.' I hesitate, then decide to accept one last call to the bathroom.

Finally towards ten, everybody arrives more or less at once. Squash partners from my Hammersmith club, a few blokes from karate classes, couples we met on the maternity course and perhaps went out with once, or used to meet for a drink sometimes, at least until Hilary was born. Mark and Sylvia, our old neighbours from Finchley. People from work. People from school where Shirley taught – her ex amongst them? Stout Ian Perkins has a lecherous look to him, trailing a petite wife with pink rabbitty little mouth and pursed lips. And now there's a faint aroma of dope in the air? Who? Can I allow that? If the police should come before I start the fire? Calm down please. It would be madness to make a fuss. Probably I'm just imagining it.

Mrs Harcourt arrives, bringing a sprightly older man with middle European accent who seems determined to make a fool of himself telling jokes and drinking heavily. He is tall, but lean, over-dressed in a dinner jacket that doesn't quite fit. Obviously out for a good time. Mrs Harcourt introduces him, with no comment, as her dear friend Jack. She is looking younger and happier than the last time I saw her, in an elaborate taffeta dress with sparkling butterfly brooch and pearl necklace. I'm surprised to notice she hasn't brought her camera. Our tenth anniversary will pass unrecorded.

Gregory turns up with a girl I've never seen before, a thin-lipped, depressed looking lass with a sudden false smile of greeting that heaves up the downturned corners of the mouth. Tight jeans and ample curves up top tell all though. She moves with a soft predatory pad in expensive running shoes.

'Divorced, old man,' he explains. It's at least two years since I saw him. The girl is leaning over the table for food and he is watching her arse. So am I for that matter. He chuckles:

'Just got too much. And boring into the bargain. You know, marriage, always the same. We both wanted out.'

As I open the door for someone else, Charles and Peggy can be heard arguing quite violently as they approach down our lovely, tree-waving street. They are calling each other names. Sometimes I wonder if Shirley and I aren't the only couple in the world guarding the romantic fort of first marriage.

Lobster Claws

'Hi, what you up to? How come we never get to see each other?' Greeting guests in the porch I'm putting on an extraordinary show of bonhomie: I sound positively American. Meanwhile Shirley is marshalling drinks and food in the breakfast room. In the lounge somebody's put on 'Street-Fighting Man' of all things. I check my watch. Ten fifteen.

'Congratulations,' I tell a very pregnant Susan Wyndham; she is leaning on the arm of the bearded man whose photo I used to see in her bedroom. 'What do you want, boy or a girl?'

'Just as long as it's healthy,' he says solemnly.

The evening gathers momentum. Much as planned. People finally begin to mingle, to get drunk. And to dance. The volume of the music is creeping up, and with the noise comes bustle, confusion. I've spotted several cigarette butts on carpet and parquet and a glass of red wine has gone over the bottom of the heavy green velvet curtains in the lounge. Pretty expensive enjoyment frankly. What I can't understand, though, is how Shirley, who has committed so much time and energy in recent years to cleaning everything up far more often than is necessary ('because Hilary spends most of her life on the carpet'), is now being so blasé about it all. 'Oh that doesn't matter, I'm sure the stain'll come out. We're not that finicky. I mean, you can't live in a museum, can you?' She lifts her hand to cover her laughter, embraces someone, whirls off in a dance.

Still, the louder and rowdier the party, the better it suits my purpose. And I break open a couple of fresh packs of

Rothmans and spill the cigarettes into a cut-glass bowl on the sideboard. The lounge is already a smog. When they're always telling you on the news that everybody's giving up.

Where's Mother? I expected she'd have gone by now. Got one of the 'church folk' to drive her home. But she hasn't said goodbye. I don't want her around when it all happens. There are two rather handsome people kissing deeply at the bottom of the stairs. Which reminds me. I walk briskly to the back of the hall and slip into the cubby under the stairs, crouching down under the slanting ceiling. Amongst dusty boxes, there's a heavy half-full drum of varnish from when they did the floors. I shift it over to the wall on the study side (barely a yard from the armchair) and prise the lid open a little with the car keys in my pocket to release some fumes. Ideally, I would like the stairwell to go up before people realise what's going on. Though that seems a little ambitious.

Then up to check the children one last time. Fortunately the guest room is at the opposite side of the house from Hilary's. For obvious reasons. The important thing is that everybody be where they should be when it begins.

I ease open the door. Frederick has his arms flung out above his head in red pyjamas. His face is so smooth in sleep, despite the thumping rhythm from downstairs, so smooth, so calm. But then he doesn't have dreams like I have, like last night's for example. I watch him. Although they don't actually move you can sense, beneath the calm features, an intense, fluttering, delicate life. Not for the first time I reflect that I too might have had a lovely child like this.

Where the hell is Mother? I don't want her holed up in a bedroom somewhere praying. That would be typical. And I quickly move along the two passageways that meet at right angles at the top of the stairs, opening doors, checking the bedrooms, the linen cupboard, the bathroom, even the tiny laundry room. Which paranoid activity inevitably reminds me of last night's dream again, and I pause a moment at the top of the stairs as it all comes back.

I knew it had been a bad one. Of course, essentially, it's just the same old mutilation fare. The new twist being that this time I was looking for my face. All over the house opening doors, looking under furniture, searching for my face. Unusually, though, as anxiety mounted, as I desperately hunted for and equally desperately hoped I wouldn't find my nose, my eyes, my mouth, and worse still the expression those features must form, I came across Shirley brushing her hair in the bathroom the way she does, tossing it this way and that with a lovely sensuous motion. Instinctively I lifted my hands to cover myself, but she says calmly, 'Nothing wrong with your face, love,' and immediately I'm calm too. At least no one has noticed, I think, so perhaps it doesn't matter. One can perfectly well go through life without a face if nobody notices. But now she frowns: 'You really should get your arms looked at though, George.' As though changing slides on a projector, attention switches in a flash to my right arm where strange pink rubbery outcroppings of flesh are forming just beneath the shoulder. I run a finger across them. 'Age,' I say, in the way one might of the dry fatty skin one tends to get above the elbow. But these jelly-like protrusions are gross. And then I see my forearms. They are bristling, bristling, with long, maybe four-inch lobster claws, blackish, as if burnt, unutterably ugly as they wave and grope of their own accord. I open my mouth to scream. To find I haven't a mouth, for there is no face of course. At which point one wakes up to find that all is perfectly okay.

Downstairs I check out the lounge. Maybe fifteen people. Almost everybody is busy dancing or at least deep in conversation. Gregory's girlfriend is writhing particularly wildly, though always stony-faced. Very suggestive contortions, and not near Gregory either. No sign of Shirley, or Mother. Where is she? In the breakfast room Charles is at the buffet table with a leg of chicken in his mouth, defending Liverpool local council against the robust good sense of Susan's man, Eric. One of the karate guys splits his trousers showing how important it is to assume a low centre of gravity.

There is something very stable about the hum now, as if this buzz of alcohol-fuelled voices will go on for many hours. And checking my watch it is indeed time. I planned to do it now, when in the general tipsy hubbub Hilary will be forgotten. Sensing that if I stop to think, the cold sweat which is already coating face and hands will turn into violent shivering, I move to the sideboard where the spirits are. A well-dressed, clean-shaven boy who doesn't know who I am, offers to do me the honours. 'Fill it up,' I tell him. He grins as if at a fellow freeloader. I take a gulp, light myself a cigarette, and armed, as it were, to the teeth, push through people down the hall, down the passage by the stairs, round through the cloakroom, past the bathroom and the door to the cubby and into the secluded study room.

To find Peggy and Gregory.

Why, after my silly, automatic, 'Oops, sorry,' closing the door on them, do I have such an overwhelming sense of frustration, and more precisely of *déjà vu*? My childhood. Hearing, finding, knowing of Peggy with her lovers, feeling excluded, feeling somehow that my bubbly sister has a monopoly on life, on gaiety, that I am always to be in outer darkness gnashing my teeth. It's only a couple of months since she had her abortion for heaven's sake.

I hesitate in the cloakroom where hooks are overloaded with rain-scented jackets, duffles, macs, mohair. In the bathroom someone coughs. An explosion of laughter comes from just round the corner in the hall. My cigarette is more than half burned. I take a good gulp of the whisky, knock brusquely on the study again and push back in.

'George, really!'

'Sorry, I don't want to bother you guys, but Charles is looking all over for you, Peg. Could walk in any moment.'

They're still at the stage of fumbling in each other's clothes. They only met at most a couple of hours back. They both came with other partners. Gregory half sits, flustered, a glint of saliva on his beard.

'Why don't you, er, adjourn a moment and nip upstairs. Go to our room at the end of the passageway to the right. There's a key in the door.'

But our room is next to Hilary's room. Why on earth did I suggest this? Do I want them to burn? Or do I want them

169

to save Hilary? In which case, what's the point? Or was it the only thing I could think of? In any event I'm screwing up. I'm losing control. I draw the last puffs on the cigarette with my black lobster claws and tip another gulp of whisky into the place where my mouth must be. Only half the glass left.

'Good on you, bruv,' Peg says chuckling. The two of them are getting up, rearranging their clothes. 'We'll run the gauntlet of the hall then.' And crouching down, like a commando about to storm a beach she grabs gangly Gregory by the hand and begins to hurry out through the cloakroom.

I look around. They've turned on the angle lamp on the desk, pointing it down at the floor near the wall. And in this would-be romantic, shadowy light, I quickly toss my whisky onto a dusty green armchair, then dislodge the dying coal of my cigarette so that it falls at the edge of the little pool of yellow spirit seeping into the cushion. Immediately it goes out. Without hesitating I pull a lighter from my pocket and try to light the material directly. An almost invisible paraffin flame appears, but seems not to touch the material itself, seems to dance, detached and ghostlike. It surely can't be enough. But I must get out now. I can't wait to see. I haven't even closed the door properly. I turn to grab the ashtray I left on the desk and spill it over the flame. But it isn't there. Why? Why not? Has some creepy person like my mother already gone round gathering and emptying ashtrays? For heaven's sake!

The flames are biting into the material now, the metamorphosis of fire is taking place, flaring yellow and smoky. I should put the thing out at once. Any forensic idiot will be able to see it was started on purpose. But in a trance I move to the door. And at last I realise, with the sudden lucidity of revelation that I am only acting here and now so that some action in my life at last there may be. So that I won't keep plaguing myself trying to decide what to do. The outcome is almost irrelevant. I am acting because I can't bear myself. I find my mental processes intolerable. I am horrible. And I may very well just go upstairs and sit out the horror with Hilary, burn away my lobster claws, my

170

jelly flesh. My mother is right. I have been damned from earliest infancy.

The light of the flames is now brighter and fiercer than that of the lamp. I must have been here five minutes. There's the fierce crackle of a bonfire. Suddenly frightened by the common-sense fear that somebody will hear, will smell, I hurry out of the room and close the door carefully behind me. The heavy wood clicks softly on good do-it-yourself insulating foam. And in an unplanned brainwave I go and pick up the low table at the bottom of the hall, bring it back, set it down across the study door and, unburdening the hooks one by one, place a huge pile of damp coats on top. Now back to the party. My face, I feel, like Moses returning from Sinai, is glowing with heat.

Help Me

'You're wanted in the lounge.'

I've barely turned the corner out of the cloakroom when I run into one of the church folk Shirley introduced me to earlier. The word 'wanted' frightens me. I would have washed my face if only the bathroom was empty.

'Oh really. Thanks.'

I meant to hang around chatting in the hall at this point until the fire was discovered, then rush upstairs, save Frederick and report that Hilary's room is already engulfed in flame. Can I spare a moment?

'Hey, George,' Charles calls through a group of talkers. 'There you are. You're wanted in the lounge.'

I'll have to go. I cross the hall and start to walk across the parquet of the lounge, normally covered by carpets, where twenty or thirty people are dancing to African music I didn't know we had. Who wants me? Is it a trick? All at once Shirley comes across from the window end and throws her arms round me in celebratory embrace. 'George, where've you been? Everybody's waiting for you!'

People dancing part about us. It's like a scene from a film. Or a dream. It feels orchestrated. And Shirley has changed. She's wearing a short black dress with glitter, the skirt pleating out high on her thighs, black tights with a zig-zag pattern, silver heels. Her hair is up with just two copper ringlets falling round each temple. A lot of make-up makes her look younger than I ever expected to see her again. I realise I haven't really looked at her all evening. She must be mad at me.

She does a twirl, a pirouette, the motion lifting her skirt, then grabs me in a tight hug. Apparently this is prearranged because the music stops now and everybody cheers. But my ears are straining for some sound behind this sound. One of the school crowd, a small, smug, balding man in cord jacket and jeans, throws handfuls of confetti over us. Everybody's clapping. 'Give the girl a kiss,' a voice shouts. But it's Shirley kissing me, twining tight to me. I try to return some passion. Thankfully, the stereo crackles, starts, stops – somebody is having trouble with the faulty cueing device – then settles into 'As Times Roll By', or whatever it's called. The appropriate guff, but loud enough to cover anything behind I think. Everybody is crowding into the room for the celebrations. Nobody will notice anything.

Tears glistening in her wide eyes, an extraordinary yearning look on her face, Shirley whispers: 'Shall we dance?' Her voice conveys infinite tenderness and irony. It's a voice that says, 'Despite everything, George, here we are, so we may as well celebrate.' She begins to lead me in a slow lilting embrace.

Am I crying? I register such intense alarm. What am I doing? She hasn't guessed the slightest thing. If she knew, if she knew even what I dreamt last night she might never touch me again. She might sense the lobster arms, the cancerous jelly protrusions.

Instead here she is being very sexy, pressing her whole slim body against me, her small breasts. The guests part into two lines forming an aisle down the lounge as we drift in slow and frankly clumsy rotation toward the fireplace end where a huge cake has appeared on a glass trolley. Behind it stands my mother, knife in hand, beaming almost tangible sentimentality. I recognise at once her Christmas cake recipe from Gorst Road days, it will be full of a pension's worth of dry fruit and suet. Though instead of the usual Mary, Joseph and Jesus plus farmyard friends in adoration, another holy family are standing on the icing: three figures, toy figures, cuddly bears but dressed as human. There's Daddy with a peaked railwayman's cap, Mummy

173

in an apron, and little girl. Us. Except that the child is standing up.

I glance at my watch. How long has it been?

A sudden hush. Mother pushes a knife into the cake. 'Bless you, my dears,' she says. 'Many happy returns.' Charles pops a champagne bottle. He says, 'Good on you, George lad,' in a fake downwardly-mobile voice. Shall I tell him that Peggy is having it off with Gregory upstairs? Around the happy figures on the cake, in rose-pink icing, Mother's shaky hand has traced with how much love, '10TH ANNIVERSARY'. Loud cheers go up with the first splashing of champagne. Everyone crowds round to kiss and squeeze.

Then someone cries: 'Speech, speech from the happy couple.'

'Speech!'

A slow handclap begins: 'Speech, speech, speech.'

My house is burning.

Shirley says: 'Go on, George!'

I can feel the muscles in my face working. What is happening? Why has nobody said anything? Obvious. Because everybody is in the room here, looking at me. It couldn't have been more perfectly timed. The jostle of glasses, plates of cake moving round, jokes, red faces, comments. Two or three flashes pop.

Frederick. I must hurry. Unless it has already gone out. Just say something and get it over with. Say something.

'Oh come on, George.'

Why can't I *speak*!

'Tongue-tied by love.'

'Give the man a drink.'

'Spoilsport!'

My mother says: 'Come on, love.'

And now I am perfectly aware that I am breaking down. This is what it is like, then. I open my mouth, but nothing comes out. My whole body surges with damp nervous heat. My bowels are melting. I gaze at all these faces, eager, grinning. They find my bewilderment so touching. Probably all I have to say is thank you, thank you, for this wonderful surprise. But I feel my jaws locked, paralysed. They will not speak. I can sense tears rolling down numbed cheeks. Until finally I manage to croak, 'Help me.'

But nobody hears; my whispered plea is drowned in a fierce yell from the door: 'Fire! There's a bloody great fire. Everybody out.'

An Act of Goodness

I should say, if for no other reason than not to appear ridiculous, that I always knew my plan was a risky one, that it could perfectly well have an entirely different outcome from the one I intended. Or, most probably, no outcome at all. At the time I reasoned that this was precisely why I was choosing it. In this sense: that no one with only moderate insurance and no financial problems could ever be suspected of arson against his own household; and second, that no one could ever be suspected of a murder attempt when the outcome was so spectacularly uncertain and in circumstances where so many people might, theoretically, rush upstairs to save the handicapped child who couldn't save herself. That said, however, I felt fairly confident that in the selfish tipsy hubbub that is a party around midnight, the general reaction to a fire that in the secluded back study under cover of the thump of music and a haze of cigarette smoke ought to be well advanced before being discovered, would be to panic and rush to get out.

I was worried, of course, about Shirley and Mother. It was unlikely they would forget the little girl. Which was why I'd much rather Mother had never been invited, or had gone home early. But my idea was that I, being mentally prepared and well placed at the foot of the stairs, would shout commandingly to the others to stay down and dial 999 while I went up for the children. Given that Hilary's room was directly above the study, given that both windows would be open, given that curtains are reasonably inflammable, and given above all that I would have the excuse of going for Frederick first, I very much hoped that on arrival in her

176

room the child would be beyond saving, already liberated I liked to put it to myself, and why not for heaven's sake?, from the prison of her body. I would rush down with Frederick only seconds before the staircase was engulfed in flames from burning varnish beneath, and by the time the fire brigade arrived all would be over.

Looking back now, I realise that this schoolboy-fantasy scenario was never really entirely probable, for who can know where or how fast a fire will spread? Nor in the end perhaps was it why I had decided to act as I did.

The voice shrieked fire, a voice I didn't recognise. The reaction of this party crowd, these people we had sought out for this improbable celebration, was, as expected, first confusion, then a strong fast surge to the door. My problem was that I should have been at the foot of the stairs, ready. In the event, as I threw myself into the crowd, screaming, 'The children, the children!' it was to feel the whole house suddenly shudder; a deep crash rumbled the walls and a blast of hot air rushed to meet the fleeing party guests. Perhaps the place wasn't as well built as the estate agents had led me to believe.

Desperately forcing my way, and being forced in turn, through urgent bodies out into the hall, I found the stairs already invaded by quick low flames. How could that be? At the same moment all electric light – this I had never even thought of – went out, throwing the whole scene into a lurid flickering relief that was simultaneously bright and dark. Looking up, aghast, disaster dawning, I saw my mother at the halfway landing where, behind candlestick columns of polished oak, the staircase turned. Incongruously she had lifted her long satiny party dress to hurry through fire licking across blue carpeting. As she scuttled round the corner out of vision, three or four stairs on the main flight crashed down in a fierce spouting of sparks and flame. The varnish, it seems, had been something of an excess of zeal. The armchairs must have been veritable incendiary devices. They shouldn't be allowed. In any event, the scene, as I backed off from the heat, was lost in a billow of dark smoke and cinders, chokingly hot. And I paused.

Shirley grabbed me from behind in hysterics. She was shrieking. I didn't turn to her. Now the drama had begun in earnest and so much was at stake, I found myself quite cool in that heat and thinking so rapidly.

The last of the guests were forcing their way out of the front door. Telling Shirley to follow me, I crossed the hall to breakfast room and kitchen, suddenly almost normal after the choking bonfire of the stairway. I sensed a curious adrenalin-filled togetherness as we dashed through the twilit spectre of our domestic life, a table laden with dirty dishes and party snacks, a black gleam from the door of the microwave. She reached for my hand. I pulled her along, shouting commands which she obeyed. So in just a few moments we were out through the side door, had opened the garage, pulled out the light aluminium ladder there and were stumbling to the house through flowerbeds and rockery to prop it wobbling against the wall below Frederick's window. It will be quicker, I tell her, to cross the house once in, than to walk the ladder round to Hilary's room.

How gloriously instinctively one acts. Without knowing where I've picked it up, I find, as I climb the ladder Shirley holds, that I have a hammer in my hand. Though it does occur to me as odd that Freddy hasn't opened the window himself.

The top of the ladder is three feet short of the sill. Hammer clamped between my teeth I place my hands flat against the gritty brick, hugging the wall, and very precariously raise my feet to the second-to-top rung. Shirley shouts encouragement, begs me to hurry. 'George, George, please!' But her noise comes as if from a distant television. I am not listening to her. Extraordinarily lucid, what my mind is actually registering as my hand comes down with the hammer on polished glass, is that there is now a wavering glow sharpening the edges of the house to either side, that as yet there is no sound of a fire engine, that a group of guests are gathering at the base of the ladder.

The glass shatters. My hand reaches in for the catch. At the same time I'm shouting down that no one else should come up. I can handle it. And in the distance I distinctly hear Charles voice calling urgently for Peggy. Indeed. Where is she? Why haven't *they* saved the kids? I heave myself forward over the sill, tearing my shirt on the pin that holds the bar.

The small room is acrid with a slow, almost leisurely grey smoke which flaps and curls as I open the window. Frederick is not on the bed.

My mind speeds up, spacily aware. Crossing rapidly to the door, I'm shouting for Frederick at the top of my voice. 'Freddy, for Christ's sake!' No reply. Just the loudening roar of the flames. Through the door there's laundry room, another bedroom and bathroom to the left, stairs to the right. I go right, towards danger, the fire; perhaps he tried to go down the stairs. I'm calling more and more urgently, Freddy, Freddy, fighting the urge to cough, to turn back; until, advancing into ever thicker, yellowish smoke which stings my eyes and makes me retch, I stumble over him, stretched on blue pile carpet, his slight body sprawled in red pyjamas, his blond hair, outflung arms.

In only a moment, less, I have snatched him back to the open window. He weighs nothing. He's a feather. And I am sure he is alive, he must be. He can't have lain there more than a minute. How long has it all been? Not more than a minute or two, surely. He must be alive. Suddenly I find I have faith. Am I breathing a prayer? No. I just know the worst can't happen, it can't. I race through the spare room and simply pass this dear child directly into the hands of the small balding man from St Elizabeth's (my wife's ex lover?) who, disregarding my orders, is standing at the top of the ladder looking in.

It's so incongruous. As if I were living in my dreams. Or is that the key? For instead of throwing a leg over the sill and following Frederick down the ladder to safety, I stand at the window, filling my lungs, preparing to turn back, just as in my dreams I will insist on going back and back, looking and looking for that horrible thing that remains forever hidden.

I turn back. And only now in this scorching, unbreathable heat, when I could perfectly honourably retire, do I begin to appreciate why I have acted as I have. It must have been, I see as I fill my lungs at the window, it must have been to force myself, in these precious seconds of action and drama, to truly decide once and for all, and in decision to find myself, that mutilated part of me I spend my nights seeking, that missing face. At the door to Hilary's room presumably.

My chest painfully full of air, I grab the blanket from off the bed, gather it about me and run at the thickening smoke and flames at the top of the stairs, from where, forming a right angle, the other landing leads off to airing cupboard, our room, Hilary's room.

I pass through flames. Screaming inwardly, breath fiercely held, I blunder, eyes closed, along the corridor, blanket tight about my head, legs scorching. The noise has become deafening, a rage of spitting, crackling explosions above a steadily booming roar. I pass through it. Weeping. Then suddenly there are no more flames, the landing beyond the stairs is clear, though the smoke here is dense as thick wool. Another sudden crash shakes our house.

How long can I hold this breath?

I turn toward the flickering quick orange light through an open doorway to the left which must be flames in the curtains of Hilary's room (I planned for this). And I am just crossing that fatal threshold when I realise that they are already here, at the end of the landing. It was the smoke and my almost closed, burning eyes kept me from seeing them. My mother is slumped against the door to our bedroom. Her dress, her underskirt, are burnt up to the waist. Her skin is black. Despite the urgency, I experience a strange sense of revelation at the sight of her heavy vulnerable flesh. My mother. And the ragged bundle left to roll to one side, half in the airing cupboard, must be Hilary. She is motionless. I reach for the handle of our bedroom door, the only escape route, but even before I touch it I know what has happened. They locked it, Peggy and Gregory. Mother couldn't get through to take the child out.

They locked it. But why didn't they unlock it? For Christ's sake. Can they still be in there? Surely not. The roar of the fire in Hilary's room is ear-splitting. Why why why didn't they unlock that door? This is mad.

My mother stirs and groans. I can't see her face which is squashed against the angle of door and carpet. Hilary likewise is merely a mound in the swirling dark.

Has it been thirty seconds, forty, fifty, since I took this breath?

In the space of a breath, a single breath, I must decide who I am.

I look about me from stinging, streaming eyes. My generous mother. My hopeless, helpless child. My expensive, graceful, gorgeous house, burning. This is the moment of truth I have so expensively engineered. I look, but there is no revelation, no dream mirror to show me whatever my face may be, nor through the suffocating smoke do I miraculously see any missing part of me to be rushed off to that improbable surgeon. There is no help. Only unthinking, with savage violence, I begin to do my instinctive duty by these others.

Indeed my fury and aggression are their only hope now. For I cannot drag them both back through the bonfire at the top of the stairs. I know that. One perhaps, but not both. And though again I know that this is precisely the kind of situation I strove to bring about, nevertheless the simple solution of leaving that blurred bundle behind, is, for reasons beyond reason, immediately discounted now. I turn to the door, step over my mother and with the last of this interminable breath give the jerking kick I learnt long ago at karate.

The wood shudders but does not give.

Why shouldn't I just pull my mother free, back along the passage through the flames, assuming it can be done? Why am I forever thinking one thing and doing another?

I'm shaking. To regain control I begin to breathe out, slowly, slowly, from squeezed and painful lungs. And kick again. This time I yell fiercely, expelling the last of that breath in an explosion of violence, springing the kick right by the lock.

Nothing.

So now I have to, have to, take this next breath, the beginning of the rest of my life. Which may be very brief. My lungs are crushed, skewered. My vision falters. In a frenzy of frustration, I take a few paces back to where the flames are darting in glowing beads across the carpeting and, head down, I simply charge the door with my thick stubborn skull. In a shock of pain, it gives.

I grab my mother. Heaving her dead weight across the room to the window, already flung open, I register that Peggy and Gregory are not here. Insanely they have fled through the window. Did they think somebody was trying to discover them? The roof of the side porch is only five or so feet below. I could lower mother down first, then follow her myself. Mission accomplished.

For a moment I pause. Leaning over the sill, I gasp the sweet air, taking in the dark garden scene, the crowd, the shouts, the halo of a tree in blossom, the silhouette of other chimneyed houses stretching away downhill under a yellow city glow, the sudden wail of sirens. Then, against my better judgement perhaps, like my mother so many years ago when she renounced her faith for me, I go back in there and lift that small soul clear.

Epilogue

It's evening. I've been relaxing outside by the goldfish pond in the patio of our Maida Vale house. I've been taking it rather easy of late is the truth. I can't be bothered to bring work home any more. There does come a time when one realises that such things are not so important. Though it would be silly to say I should have seen this before. I'm past even blaming myself. Paper on my knees, I sit here enjoying the soft light, the summer air, the gentle back and forth of the swing couch. A skyline of chimneypots and TV aerials hardens above the ivy wall. There are blue curtains in a neighbour's bedroom and peeps of domesticity in lighted windows. I sip my gin, light a Camel. Sometimes I wonder if I haven't just discovered how to enjoy life. You know? I work hard enough, my programs are better than ever, when I come home I do my bit with dear Hilary, we chuckle together if she's in form, then in the evening I step out here to watch the coal of my cigarette brightening as the twilight bleeds away. Next week we're going to do a family holiday in south-west France.

The article I'm reading on the health service doesn't interest me. It's too strident. The guy must have some kind of problem. My eye strays, follows the cool darting goldfish between their lily leaves, the slow stream of planes that wink over west London in the dusk. I like Maida Vale. I like a way the sparrows have of scuffling in the ivy. A march of ants across the paving. And then I must have fallen asleep, since I wake now with a start and a shiver to find it's past midnight. For God's sake, I'm freezing. But deeply contented somehow. A man falling asleep on his patio; that's some achievement.

I clear up my empty glass, a bowl of peanuts, lock the doors and climb upstairs to bed. Shirley isn't there yet. She is tending Hilary through the nth tonsilitis. There are cooing noises from down the passage. I undress, lie down and have just switched out the light when I hear her feet padding to the bathroom. A few minutes later she treads quietly into the room and slips in between the sheets.

'Got her off?'

'Oh, are you still awake? Yes,' she says. 'Yes, I have.'

We lie on our backs saying nothing in the staring dark. A lorry passes on Elgin Avenue. 'Go to sleep,' I tell her, 'I'll get up if she cries. It's my turn.' Because we've worked out a fairly reasonable routine with these things now. But Shirley replies: 'She won't cry, George.'

There's something unusual in her voice, and she doesn't often use my name like that. After another moment lying still, I prop myself up on an elbow, and stare into her shadowy face. Her eyes are wide open.

'I just gave her all the medicine in the cupboard.'

She begins to explain that she couldn't help it. She started spooning in the medicine – the girl was suffering – and then felt she couldn't stop. She felt somehow the child was urging her to do it.

'It was as if I heard her voice. As if she'd been speaking to me for years. You know? I knew the voice so well. It was her. And she was saying, do it, do it now.'

Shirley is pleading, as I might have done a year or so ago in similar circumstances. She speaks softly and persuasively. But she is telling me what she knows can't be true. And she knows I know. She has said it so many times herself: how can a child who doesn't know what death is, nor that medicine might bring it about, urge you to make this gesture? But I remember my own experience, spooning in sweet syrup; that peculiar sense of rightness, the nearness of release.

'Everything,' she says, 'the whole caboodle. I've been at it half an hour. You know how long it takes to get her to swallow things.' With a simple laugh she adds: 'For what it's worth, I was praying as I did it.'